New York Times and *USA TODAY* bestselling author **Katee Robert** learned to tell her stories at her grandpa's knee. Her 2015 title *The Marriage Contract* was a RITA® finalist, and *RT Book Reviews* named it 'a compulsively readable book with just the right amount of suspense and tension'. When not writing sexy contemporary and romantic suspense she spends her time playing imaginative games with her children, driving her husband batty with *what-if?* questions, and planning for the inevitable zombie apocalypse.

If you liked *Make Me Crave*, why not try

Wild Thing by Nicola Marsh
Destroyed by Jackie Ashenden
Best Laid Plans by Rebecca Hunter

Discover more at millsandboon.co.uk

MAKE ME CRAVE

KATEE ROBERT

MILLS & BOON

First Published in Great Britain 2018
by Mills & Boon, an imprint of HarperCollins*Publishers*
1 London Bridge Street, London, SE1 9GF

© 2018 Katee Hird

ISBN: 978-0-263-93224-9

MIX
Paper from
responsible sources
FSC C007454

This book is produced from independently certified FSC™ paper
to ensure responsible forest management.
For more information visit www.harpercollins.co.uk/green.

Printed and bound in Spain
by CPI, Barcelona

**To Hunter McGrady.
You're an inspiration!**

CHAPTER ONE

"I SHOULD CANCEL." Allie Landers threw another massive load of white towels into the washer and bumped the door closed with her hip. "Honestly, I shouldn't have let you talk me into this in the first place."

"It's cute that you think you let me do anything." Her best friend, Becka Baudin, laughed. She pulled another set of shoes out of the metal bin and paired them up with the appropriate-sized cubby. "And, besides, I already checked us in for our flight. It's too late to turn back now. Our classes are covered. Claudia is handling all the administrative work for the week—for both the gym *and* the shelter. If you stay, you'll just stand around and stress out because things are operating just fine without you." She slid another set of spin shoes back into their cubby. "When's the last time you took a day off, Allie?"

Allie sighed, because that was the one argument she couldn't win. She didn't take days off. Her gym, Transcend, and the women's shelter it helped support were her life. She even lived in the apartment above the building combining the two. When she wasn't filling in teaching a class for one of the girls she employed, she was handling àdministrative work or doing whatever was required for the shelter.

She preferred it that way. Being busy made her feel complete in a way that nothing else did. She was a vital cog in a perfectly operating machine.

Except little about it was perfect these days.

The few donors she'd had who helped keep the women's shelter afloat had dried up. The gym functioned just fine on its own, but she'd been using every bit of profit to keep the shelter going. Because of that, the gym was in jeopardy now, too. The result… She was in trouble. More trouble than she'd let on to anyone. Admitting it aloud was akin to making it real, and she couldn't do that. There was a way out. There had to be.

A way that didn't involve selling out to the vulture investors who'd been circling for months. Allie just needed *time* to figure it out.

The very last thing she needed was to jet off to the Caribbean to some private island for a week. But if she admitted as much to Becka, then she'd have to admit everything else.

She couldn't. Not yet.

Allie had just sunk what remained of her personal savings account into keeping the power bill paid at the shelter, which meant another month gone by without debt collectors calling. Or, worse in so many ways, without having to turn out any of the women currently living there.

"Hello? Earth to Allie." Becka waved a hand in front of her face, a frown marring her expression. "Where'd you go?"

"Nowhere important." She forced a smile and reached over to flick her friend's hair. "The blue suits you." It was just as bright as Becka's personality, several shades melded together to create something beautiful.

"Don't change the subject." Her friend frowned harder. "You aren't going to cancel, are you? If you try, I will hog-tie you to your suitcase and haul your ass to the airport myself. You're going to relax and enjoy yourself for a week even if it kills both of us."

Allie snorted. "If it kills both of us, that's hardly relaxing, is it?"

"Smart-ass." Becka's blue eyes were pleading. "I've already left our contact info with Claudia. I promise, if something happens and they need you, I'll pay for your flight back to New York without bitching about it once. And I'll never bully you into going on vacation again."

Allie raised her eyebrows. "How much did you

have to pay Claudia to make sure she doesn't call me?" That was the only way Becka would make a promise like that. Her friend played to win, and she wasn't afraid to play dirty. Claudia was just as bad.

Becka all but confirmed it. "Claudia is on the same page as I am. We both agree that you need to get the hell away from this place for a little bit."

She sighed again, but a small part of her looked forward to seven days with no email, no phone calls, no weight of the world on her shoulders. The island had no internet access except in the main lodge, so she'd have no choice but to relax. "I guess I have to go, then."

"Yes, you do!" Becka gave a little wiggle. "Now help me get the rest of these shoes put away before your class. I'm going to pop in if it doesn't fill up. Seven days of drinking and sunning myself are going to add up quick."

Allie laughed and moved to help. She pushed away the worry and stress that had plagued her for months. It would still be here when she got back. What would it hurt to just cut loose for once in her adult life? "I'm looking forward to it." And for the first time since she'd bought the tickets, she actually meant it.

Roman Bassani glared at the pretty Chinese woman behind the counter. "You've been giving me the runaround for weeks. I know for a fact that Allie Landers is in here daily and she's actively dodging my calls. I just need to talk to her." He couldn't tender her an offer to invest in her business if he couldn't pin her down, and he'd been having a hell of a time managing that since his initial call to propose the idea. Coaxing reluctant business owners into seeing things his way was something that usually came easily for him. But Allie Landers was a slipperier quarry than he'd expected.

Apparently she'd successfully dodged him. Again.

"I'm sorry, sir." Claudia didn't look the least bit sorry. "She's out of town for the next seven days. Any business you have with her will have to wait until then."

"Out of town? Where the hell did she go? There's got to be some way to get ahold of her." He didn't actually expect Claudia to answer, but apparently needling him was too much of a temptation.

She leaned forward with a small smile. "She's on a private island with no cell service or internet. If you want to contact her before she gets back, I suggest smoke signals."

Cheeky.

He could use this. Roman plastered a disbelieving look on his face. "That's bullshit. There isn't a damn place in the Western Hemisphere without cell service or Wi-Fi, let alone without both."

"There is on West Island."

Aha. He didn't let his expression shift. "If you say so. You tell Allie to call me when she gets back."

"I'm sure she'll have you at the top of her list," Claudia said sweetly.

Roman turned without another word and stalked out of the gym. He breathed an audible sigh of relief once the door closed behind him. Everything about that place was so feminine, he couldn't walk inside without feeling like a bull in a china shop. It was more than the tiny instructors that he seemed to argue with the second he asked after the owner. There wasn't a single pink thing in sight, but the place was always packed with women.

None of that was a bad thing, but the looks they gave him—as if they expected him to go on a rampage at any moment—and the subtle flinches they made if he moved too fast... It grated. It wasn't their fault, and he applauded what Allie Landers was doing there, but their behavior left him painfully aware of how big his body was by comparison to theirs, and of the fact that no matter how carefully he spoke or how expensively he dressed, he was still a goddamn animal beneath the suit.

He didn't let anyone see it, but those women sensed it all the same.

A predator.

It didn't matter that he'd chop off his hand before he raised it to a woman or child. To them, he was a threat.

Roman cursed and started down the street. He should hail a cab, but he needed to work off his aggression more. The long strides helped clear his mind and ease his agitation, leaving nothing but cold purpose in its wake.

This Allie thought she could skip town for a week and ignore the fact that his deadline was bearing down on them. Two weeks until she had to make a decision, or other investors would make the decision for her. Normally, Roman wouldn't hesitate to play dirty, but his client wanted Allie to agree to the contract without him putting on undue pressure. *An impossible task.* He had a healthy bonus waiting for him if he could pull it off, but that was secondary. His client wanted full acquisition of the business with the shelter intact—the women in the shelter would scatter if they thought it was a hostile takeover. They trusted Allie, and they sure as fuck wouldn't trust *him*.

All of it boiled down to his needing the damn woman to go along with this buyout and he couldn't convince her to get onboard if she wasn't here.

But he had a location.

Roman fished his phone out of his pocket and did some quick searching, his frustration growing when he realized that the resort was booked for the next year straight. The website promised a discreet paradise, which translated to the staff being unwilling to move things around to accommodate him. Since giving him guest names so he could offer his own incentive was against company policy, he'd hit a dead end.

Only one thing left to do. He called his best friend, Gideon Novak. "Hey, don't suppose you have any connections with West Island in the Caribbean?"

"Hello, Roman, so nice to hear from you. I'm doing well, thank you for asking."

Roman rolled his eyes. "Yes, yes, I'm being a prick. We both know that's not going to change. The island. It's important."

The slightest of pauses on the other end wouldn't have been there if he hadn't fucked things up royally six months ago. He and Gideon were mending that bridge, but rebuilding the trust was slow going. It didn't matter that Gideon understood where Roman was coming from—Roman had still almost cost his friend the love of his life, Lucy.

Finally, clicking sounded on the other end of the phone. "I haven't dealt with the owner specifically, but I've placed two separate clients with his company and they're both still working there."

It was better than he could have hoped. "I need one of the villas."

Another pause, longer this time. "Roman, if you need a vacation, book it yourself. I'm not a goddamn travel agent."

"No shit. This isn't pleasure—it's business. I need to find a guest arriving today. And offer the owner of the reservation a truly outstanding amount of money to reschedule. The resort won't give out that information to me, but if you have an in, they'll give it out to you."

"This better be *really* important."

It wasn't a question, but Roman had nothing to lose at this point. "Vitally. One of the businesses I've been trying to court for months is coming down to the deadline. If my client doesn't invest first, the other wolves circling will. They'll damage the integrity of this place and do irreparable harm to people's lives as a result."

"Sounds like you're playing the hero. A new look for you."

"Fuck no. I'm in it for the bottom line, and the bottom line is that with the right spin, this place could be making a significant amount of money, and the good press that comes from it being connected with a women's shelter would go a long way to opening doors to me that have previously been closed."

Gideon snorted. "Whatever you have to tell yourself. Give me thirty."

"Thanks."

His friend hung up without saying goodbye. Gideon would come through for him. The man was an unstoppable force, and Roman counted himself lucky to have him on his side.

Sure enough, thirty minutes later, a text came through with the reservation details—and the significant amount of money to be wired to the owner of the reservation he was co-opting. Roman wasted no time sending the money and booking the first flight out of New York.

He had seven days to track down Allie Landers and convince her to see things his way. How hard could it be on an island with only ten villas on it?

CHAPTER TWO

ROMAN TOOK FIVE minutes to change and stalk through his villa, getting a feel for the place. It was all vacation luxury, heavy on the driftwood furniture and big open spaces to maximize the view of his private beach and the foliage that surrounded three quarters of the building.

And therein lay the problem.

He should have anticipated that an island with only ten villas would play heavily into privacy, but with the various activities open to all guests, he'd anticipated there would be plenty of time to find Allie and make his argument.

He hadn't figured on not knowing which part of the island she was on.

He strode onto the beach and looked around. The natural curve of the island created a miniature bay that blocked out the view of anyone else. There were bicycles and walking paths to get to the main buildings, where there was a restaurant, a bar, a yoga studio and a boutique gift shop. He could hang out there and hope like hell that Allie would venture in for a meal, but with the option to have dining brought to the villas, he didn't like his odds.

No, better to get the lay of the land and plan accordingly.

A quick examination of the storage unit right off the sand—designed to look like a weathered shack—gave him the answer. There was gear for a variety of water sports. He considered his options and went with the kayak. It was the fastest way to get where he needed to go and stay relatively dry in the process. He shucked his shoes off, paused and then dragged off his shirt, too. The summer sun should have made the heat unbearable, but as he pushed the kayak into the water, it was damn near pleasant.

Roman hadn't been on a kayak before, but it seemed easy enough. He experimented in paddling until he got a good rhythm, then set off, heading south around the island. He'd make a circuit and go from there.

The main problem lay in the fact that he didn't exactly know who he was looking for. He'd never managed to pin Allie Landers down into meeting him in person. The digging he'd done online had brought up precious little—both in details about her as an individual and pictures of her. Her social media accounts were both set to private, and the one photo he'd found of her was from ages ago. The Transcend website, which revealed more about the company's services and vision than its founder, didn't give more information than a contact email address. Considering it was linked with a women's shelter, *that* wasn't surprising, but it still irked him.

That said, Roman had secured deals in the past that began with even less information than he had now. He was confident he'd pull it off this time, too.

The first villa to the south had a family with two smallish children making sandcastles, so Roman kept going, starting to enjoy himself despite the fact that he much preferred the city to anything resembling nature. This didn't feel like *nature*, though.

It felt a whole lot like paradise.

He made his way around the island, surveying beach by beach. There were two with families, two with groups that seemed to consist solely of men, three empty and one with a group of four women who catcalled him as he paddled past. He filed that information away to check on later. There was no telling how many friends Allie had come down here with, but he knew she wasn't married and had no children, so at least he'd narrowed down the search.

By the time he came around the north point of the island, he was fucking exhausted. Roman spent time in the gym regularly, but the heat and the constant paddling wore on him. He steered around the outcropping of rocks and let his paddle rest across the kayak in front of him, taking a moment to roll his shoulders.

Which was right around the time he saw the woman.

She lay on her back, her arms stretched over her head, her long blond hair stark against the vivid red of her beach towel. But that wasn't what made his breath dry up in his lungs.

It was the fact she was topless.

Her golden skin glinted in the sunlight as if she'd oiled herself before coming out to the beach, and the only thing resembling clothing she wore was a tiny triangle of indeterminable color. Her long legs bent as she shifted, her large breasts rising and falling with a slow breath.

He forgot what he was there for. Forgot that his muscles were damn near shaking with exhaustion. Forgot everything but his sudden need to see what color her nipples were.

What the fuck are you doing?

He shook his head. Going closer was inappropriate. Fuck, sitting there and staring like a goddamn creep was the height of inappropriate. It didn't matter how mouthwatering her curves were or the fact that she'd propped herself up on her elbows to watch him.

Roman took a deep breath, and then another. It did nothing to quell his raging cockstand, but he managed to pick up the paddle and keep rowing. Whoever that woman was, no matter that he wanted to spend a whole lot of time up close and personal with her…she wasn't Allie. The one picture he'd managed to source of the woman alone was several years old. Her goddamn senior yearbook photo. She'd been skinny to the point of being unhealthy with her hair chopped short and dyed pitch-black.

He highly doubted she looked anything like that currently.

The one defining characteristic of the women who staffed Transcend was that they were all tiny and chiseled and didn't have a soft spot on their bodies. Beautiful, yes. Roman could appreciate all body types, but none of them had made his hands shake the same way that woman on the beach did. Soft and curvy and with breasts he ached to get his mouth on.

Knock that shit off. You aren't here to fuck anyone, no matter how sexy she is. You're here for business.

He'd go to dinner tonight and see if he could sniff out which of the women on the island was Allie and make his plan from there.

And if he saw the mystery woman once he'd gotten the rest of it figured out?

Roman grinned. Maybe he'd make an exception to his rule and indulge in some pleasure along with business.

He was in paradise, after all.

"How are you doing, sweetie?" Allie pulled on a sundress and headed over to check on Becka. Her friend had indulged a little too heavily on the vodka on the flight down from the city, and the short plane ride from Miami to West Island had made her sick. She'd spent the afternoon sleeping it off, but she still looked a bit green around the gills.

Becka managed a shaky smile. "I think vodka and I broke up."

"It's temporary." She hesitated. "Do you want me to stay? Nurse you back to health?" She was pleasantly tired, but the draw of tonight's menu was enough to have her itching to ride to the lodge and get a better lay of the land. Becka had been so out of sorts when they arrived, it had been a rush to get checked in and settled in the villa so she could sleep off the worst of it.

"God, no. It's bad enough that I've brought shame on my family for ruining the first day of your desperately needed vacation. I'm not going to let you spend any time paying for my bad decisions. Go. Eat delicious food. Drink."

Allie still didn't move for the door. "Why don't I see if the chef can make up some broth or something easy on your stomach?"

"Go, go, go. You're on vacation. You're not required to mother me." She softened the words with a smile, still looking queasy.

Allie went. Becka wouldn't thank her for staying and would only feel guilty if she did, which would distract her from resting. Tomorrow would be soon enough for them to go exploring and try out the stand-up paddleboards Allie had eyed when she'd checked out the beach.

Her face heated at the fact she'd been caught sunbathing topless. Whoever that guy was, he'd been far off enough that she couldn't clearly see his face. Those shoulders, though… Allie shivered. Even at a distance, she'd seen the cut of his muscles and how purposefully he'd maneuvered the kayak through the turquoise waters. The island must have already gone to her head, because she'd spent a truly insane moment hoping he'd come to shore so she could get a better look at him.

Maybe more than a better look.

Allie laughed at her fanciful thoughts. Vacation hookups were all well and good, but if that was what she'd wanted, she'd chosen the wrong place to go. Isolation and relaxation were the name of the game on West Island, which was exactly what she'd craved when she let Becka talk her into booking the trip. It was the exact opposite of New York and her life there.

But now she found herself wondering if maybe something *slightly* more chaotic would have been a better choice. The sun and sea had soaked into her blood and the heady feeling had her convinced anything was possible. It was only a week. The perfect length of time for a fling...

If she wasn't on a private island in the middle of the ocean without a single man in sight.

She bypassed the little golf cart that was one of the main forms of transportation here. It felt good to walk after being cooped up on the plane and then lying prone while she sunned herself. She usually taught at least one class a day at Transcend—more if she needed to cover someone else's schedule—so being inactive wasn't natural for her. It was only a mile or two to the restaurant and the day had started to cool as the sun reached for the horizon. It'd be downright pleasant tonight.

She'd make sure to wake early and attend one of the yoga classes offered, and the rest of the day would be filled with activities that would keep restlessness from setting in. There was even scuba diving available, though Allie wasn't sure she was feeling *that* adventurous. Snorkeling? Sure. Going deeper with only a tank and a few tubes between her and drowning? That would take a whole lot more convincing.

The path was cleared and well maintained to allow the carts to drive without problems, so she let her mind wander as she fell into a natural stride that ate up the distance without tiring her out. Every once in a while, the path would branch off in different directions, some heading toward other villas, some heading deeper inland. There was a small selection of hiking trails that offered tours of the history of the island.

She made it to the restaurant easily and found it practically deserted. Allie paused in the doorway, wondering if she'd misunderstood the woman who'd checked them in. Maybe it was closed?

"Looks like it's just you and me."

She jumped and spun around. The man stood a respectable distance away, but his sheer size ate up the space and made her feel closed in. She froze. *I'd recognize those shoulders anywhere.* Confirming her suspicion, his gaze slid over her body as if he was reminding himself of what she looked like with nothing but what she'd worn on the beach. She tried to swallow past her suddenly dry throat. "You."

"Me." He finally looked her in the face, and she rocked back on her heels. The man was an

Adonis. There was no other way to describe his blond perfection, from his hazel eyes to the square jaw to the cleft in his chin to the body that just wouldn't quit. He might be wearing a shirt now, but the button-down did nothing to hide his muscle definition.

He held out a wide hand with equally perfect square fingers. "Let me buy you a drink?"

"We're at an all-inclusive resort."

His lips twitched, eyes twinkling. "Have a drink with me."

Oh, he was good. Charm practically colored the air between them, and she had the inexplicable impulse to close the distance and stroke a finger along his jawline. To flick that cleft chin with her tongue.

Allie gave herself a shake. "Since we're the only ones here, it'd be silly to sit apart."

The look he gave her said he saw right through the excuse, and why not when it was pathetically flimsy? The truth was that this man was magnetic and she suspected she'd be drawn to him even in a room full of people. He waved a hand at the empty place. "Lady's choice."

"How magnanimous of you."

"I try."

She laughed and headed for the table in the middle of the small patio. There were half a dozen tables, and she picked a spot that put her back to the building and presented the best view of the ocean through a carefully curated gap in the foliage.

He eyed the view and then the chair on the other side of the table, and then he picked it up and set it adjacent to hers so they were sitting on a diagonal, rather than directly across from each other. "Nice view."

She turned to agree—and found him staring at *her*.

Allie wasn't falsely modest. Life was too short to play games with body shaming and pretending she didn't have access to a mirror. She was pretty—beautiful when she put some effort into it—but she'd given up being skinny or petite after the agony of high school, and she wasn't athletically built like some of the women at her gym. Sure, she had muscle beneath her softness, and she could keep up with the best of them in her spin classes, but she loved food just as much as she loved to sweat, and her curves reflected that. Some guys had a problem with that, though she didn't keep them around as soon as comments like "Should you really be eating that?" started.

This guy looked at her like he wanted to put her on the table and feast on *her* for dinner.

The desire stoked the flame inside her that had kindled the second she saw him. She leaned forward, checking his left hand. No ring. No tan lines, either. "What brings you to West Island?"

"It's paradise, isn't it? Who wouldn't want to come here to get away from it all?"

That wasn't quite an answer, but she was distracted by the intoxicating way his mouth moved when he spoke. *Get ahold of yourself, Allie. You're in danger of panting for him.* She took a quick drink of water that did nothing to quell the heat rising with each minute she sat next to him.

Luckily, a waiter appeared to save her from saying something truly embarrassing. He outlined the menu for the night and took their drink orders, then disappeared as quickly as he'd come.

They were in the middle of one of the most beautiful places Allie had ever seen, and she couldn't manage to tear her gaze away from this stranger. She licked her lips, every muscle in her body tensing when he followed the movement. She opened her mouth, but before she could speak, he took her hand, running his thumb over her knuckles.

The touch was innocent enough, but she felt that light movement in places that were most definitely *not* innocent. She didn't have to look down to know her nipples now pressed against the thin fabric of her sundress.

His smile was slow and sinful and promised things she never would have had the gall to ask for. "This is going to sound unforgivably forward, but what do you say we get out of here and go back to my villa?"

It was crazy. More than crazy. She didn't even know his name, and she sure as hell didn't know anything more pertinent about him.

But there on the softly lit patio with the tropical scent of some flower she didn't recognize and the soft shushing sound of the tide coming in, she didn't feel like Allie, gym owner and mother hen, the responsible one who could never afford to do anything out of line or make a misstep because too many lives depended on her.

Here, she was just Allie, a woman. A woman who desperately wanted the man staring at her mouth as if he was doing everything in his power to keep from kissing her right then and there. She licked her lips again, secretly delighting in the way a muscle in his jaw jumped. "Yes."

"Yes?"

"Yes, let's get out of here."

CHAPTER THREE

ROMAN TOOK THE woman's hand as they left the candlelit restaurant and made their way to the golf cart he'd driven there. He'd considered walking, but he was so goddamn glad now that he hadn't.

She looked even better up close than she'd been on the beach. Her white floral dress displayed her large breasts to perfection, hugging her ribs and then flaring out to swish around her thighs as she walked next to him. Her long blond hair was a mass of waves tumbling just past her shoulders, and he could picture it all too easily tangling between his fingers as he thrust into her.

Slow down.

He took a careful breath, and then another, focusing on keeping his stride unhurried and his hand loose on hers. Roman was hardly a saint, but he'd never had a reaction to a woman on such an intrinsic level like he was having now. He wanted to kiss her pouty lips and run his hands over her body and...

Slow. Down.

Not happening.

Not when she looked at him from under thick lashes, her blue eyes devouring the sight of him. She wanted this.

But he had to be sure.

He pulled her into his arms when they stopped next to the golf cart. She stepped against him easily—eagerly—and he let himself off the leash enough to run his hands down her back and to cup her ass, bringing her flush against him. Her breasts pressed against his chest, and he had to bite back a groan at how good she felt. "I'm going to kiss you now."

She didn't give him the chance to follow through. She tilted her face up and captured his mouth. It was chaste as such things went, her lips soft against his, but it didn't stay that way. Roman slid one hand up to cup the back of her head and deepened the kiss, tracing the seam of her lips with his tongue and delving inside when she opened for him. Her hands fisted the front of his shirt, pulling him closer even as her hips rolled against his.

Roman tore his mouth from hers. "Golf cart. Now." Or he was in danger of forgetting where they were and fucking her right here. Even ignoring the glaring lack of a condom, he wasn't a beast incapable of anything resembling control, and this beautiful wanting woman deserved better than to be bent over a goddamn golf cart.

At least for the first time.

First time? You're out of your damn mind.

He picked her up and set her on the golf cart, enjoying the way her lips parted in a surprised O. He was showing off and he didn't give two fucks about it, especially not when he slid behind the wheel, fired up the cart and started down the path leading toward his villa. He almost asked about hers, but just because she was alone didn't mean she was *alone*.

The thought brought him up short. He glanced at her. "Are you here with someone?"

"Just my friend." She correctly interpreted his expression. "I'm single. No boyfriend. No husband."

Thank fuck. "Same." He pressed the accelerator again. There were little eco-friendly lights scattered along the edge of the path to keep them from driving into a tree, and he made it back to his villa in record time.

Roman shut off the engine and turned to face her. "I—"

"Wait." She pressed a finger to his lips, and he instinctively nipped her lightly. Her eyes went wide. "Let's just…enjoy this. It's not like it's real life. It's the fantasy of this place." She motioned with her free hand.

He couldn't argue that, not with the low sound of some bird in the distance and the sky and sea fading from magnificent colors to true dark even as they sat there. He'd left on a scattering of lights in the villa, and he took her hand and led her inside. "Hot tub?"

"Maybe later."

There was no mistaking the intent in the way she watched him, so he didn't waste time. This was, after all, the fantasy. Roman embraced that and ignored the part of him that was curious about who this woman was and why she'd come to this place. About what her life was like wherever she spent her normal time. About a lot of things. He set it aside, because he craved another taste of her, and if he started talking about shit that didn't matter, he would ruin this perfect feeling of breathless need between them.

He led her into the main bedroom. It played up the island fantasy just as much as the rest of this place did: big windows overlooking the water, a massive mattress framed by a driftwood headboard. The white comforter was ridiculously fluffy, but he wanted to see her stretched out on top of it while he drove into her.

Slow, damn it.

Roman turned and framed her face with his

hands. He kissed her, exploring her mouth as he took them deeper. She made a little helpless noise in the back of her throat that had his cock hardening even further. He licked along her neck and nudged off the strap of her dress before working his way across her upper chest to do the same to the other side.

As much as he wanted to rip the goddamn thing off her, he dragged his mouth over the swell of one breast and then the other, shifting the fabric lower with each pass. Her fingers tangled in his hair, and she arched to meet his mouth, her breath coming as quickly as his.

He captured one nipple, sucking hard until her back bowed and she let loose a little cry. "I'm taking this off."

"Good." She shimmied out of the dress in a move that made his mouth water, her breasts bouncing a little.

And then she stood before him in only a pair of pink lace panties.

"Fucking perfection," he breathed.

It was hard to tell in the low light, but a flush might have appeared on her cheeks and chest. "Don't make a girl stand here while you stare."

He shook his head, trying to clear it. "Give a man a few seconds to enjoy the view. I didn't get a chance to on the beach earlier today." He kneeled before her and ran his hands up her legs, enjoying the feel of her muscles flexing beneath his touch. He stopped at the generous curve of her hips and hooked his fingers into the edges of the panties. "It drove me fucking crazy that I didn't know the color of your nipples." The answer was a dusky rose, the contrast between her nipples and her tanned skin drawing him farther up onto his knees so he could see her better, could lick her there again.

She shook, just a little. "You could have come to find out."

"Mmm." He kissed her soft stomach as he drew her panties down her legs. "If I had, you would have run screaming up the beach and barricaded the door."

"Maybe." Her breath hitched as he ran his tongue around her belly button. "Or maybe I would have waded out into the water to meet you."

The image hit him with the force of a train. Of the waves cresting up to tease her breasts as she stood there waiting for him. Of him pulling her into his arms the same way he had here in the villa. Of her wrapping her legs around his waist and him tugging her bikini bottom to the side and— "Fuck, maybe I'll make another circuit around the island tomorrow and we can do it right."

She laughed softly. "Or maybe you can put that

wicked mouth to good use and we can focus on the here and now."

That sounded even better. Roman moved, hitching one of her legs over his shoulder, and buried his face in her pussy.

Allie had half convinced herself that she was dreaming, but the feeling of his mouth latching on to the most secret part of her was all too real. She closed her eyes and gave herself over to his licks, long and slow as if relishing her taste and feel. It was the single hottest thing she'd ever experienced.

Right up until he turned them and toppled her onto the massive bed. She gasped, the sound morphing into a moan when he pushed a single finger into her, as slow and exploring as his mouth had been.

His eyes drank in the sight of her in a move she swore she could feel. He lingered on her thighs and pussy, hips and stomach, taking extra care over her breasts, before finally settling on her face. "Perfection," he said again.

"You're not too shabby yourself." She reached over her head to grip the comforter, knowing full well that it offered her breasts up for him.

He made a sound perilously close to a growl. "Thanks." A second finger joined the first, and he barely gave her time to adjust to that before he pushed a third into her. Stretching her. Readying her. "Fuck, woman, you feel good."

"You…too." She fought to keep her eyes open, to not miss a single second of the experience. This golden god looked at her as if he wanted to imprint himself over every inch of her, and she was more than happy to play sacrifice for the night. If he could bring such pleasure with his hands and mouth, there was no telling what he'd do with the rest of his body.

He twisted his wrist so that his thumb slid over her clit with each stroke of his fingers, the combined sensation leaving her feeling warm and melty. She let go of the comforter to reach up and cup his chiseled jaw. "I'm going to call you Adonis."

He barked out a laugh. "I'm hardly that pretty."

"You're even prettier." She never would have said it in real life, without the island and pleasure making her drunk on him. Allie traced her thumb over his bottom lip, slightly fuller than the top. "You call me perfect, but you're flawless."

Another laugh, this one strained. "Trust me, I have more than my fair share of flaws." He turned his head and kissed her palm. "But we'll pretend that's not the truth tonight."

"Works for me." She didn't ask about his flaws. That wasn't what this was. She didn't even know his name, which somehow made the whole situation hotter—because Allie never did this. Ever.

Tonight she was going to.

With that thought buoying her, she reached for his pants. "I need you."

"You have me." He pushed his fingers deeper as if to demonstrate.

"No, I *need* you." She managed to get his belt off and shoved his shorts down his narrow hips. His cock was just as perfect as the rest of him, long and thick, and she swallowed hard. "I'm tired of waiting."

"That's too damn bad, because I'm just getting started." He slid his fingers out of her and looped an arm beneath her waist, sliding her farther onto the bed until he could place her hands on the bottom of the headboard. "I'm not going to tie you down."

Her heart tried to beat itself out of her chest at the thought. "I don't know how I'd feel about that." *Liar.* She wanted it. Allie didn't think she was particularly kinky before tonight, but the thought of being at the mercy of this man…

Slow your roll. He's a stranger. Getting tied up by a stranger is a bad idea, even in paradise.

He stopped, kneeling above her on all fours, his cock dipping down until it almost touched her stomach. Those hazel eyes were completely serious for the first time since she'd met him. *An hour ago. You met him an hour ago.*

He didn't touch her, though he was close enough that she could feel the warmth coming off his body. "If you've changed your mind, we can stop. I'll give you a ride back to your villa or, if you aren't comfortable with that, you can take the cart and the staff will return it to me tomorrow." No judgment in his tone. No trying to guilt her or pull some shady business. Just ensuring that this was exactly where she wanted to be.

She gripped the headboard. "I want to stay. I want you."

His grin had her breath fluttering in her chest like a trapped thing. "You won't regret it."

Before she could think too hard about what tomorrow would bring, he kissed her, long and slow. Reacquainting himself with her as if it had been days since they'd last touched instead of moments. Her Adonis worked his way down her body one torturous inch at a time, turning parts of her erogenous that she never would have considered before that night. The inside of her elbow. The bottom of her ribs. Her knees.

He stroked and kissed her body as if memorizing every inch, until she was a quivering mess. Her world narrowed down to where he would touch her next, to the only parts of her he *hadn't* touched—her breasts and the spot between her thighs where she ached for him. "Please. Adonis, please."

He chuckled against her inner thigh, and she felt it like a bolt to her pussy. "I like it when you call me that."

"I'll call you anything you want if you just *touch* me."

"I *have* been touching you." He shifted to lay next to her, his big palm coasting over her body, an inch off her skin. She shook with the need to arch up and feel him, but the slant of his brows told her that if she tried, he'd just move his hand farther from her. "Unless you mean something specific. Like here." His fingers drifted just above her nipples and then down until she could feel the air displacement above her clit. "Or here."

"Please."

The touch was so light, she thought she might have imagined it. But she didn't imagine the look in his hazel eyes. He leaned down until his lips brushed hers with each word. "I want to feel you coming on my cock."

CHAPTER FOUR

ROMAN HAD LAUGHED when he'd found the stash
of condoms on his initial exploration of the villa,
but he'd never been so glad for them as he was in
the moment when he ripped through a foil packet
and rolled the condom over his cock.

He looked at her sprawled on his bed, her long
limbs askew, her pussy so wet he could see it glis-
tening from where he stood, her breasts reddened
from his mouth, her hair a tangle over the white
comforter... Passion personified. "Aphrodite."

She tore her gaze away from his cock. "What?"

"If I'm Adonis, then you're my Aphrodite." He
wanted to know her real name, but Roman wasn't
a fool—if he pressed her now about it, it would
ruin the fantasy they played at. He ran his hands
up her thighs as he climbed back onto the bed.
"You look like her statue."

Her lips curved in a sinful smile. "You already
have me in your bed. You don't have to go over-

board with the compliments." She leaned up on her elbows and kissed his throat. "If you don't slide your cock into me right this second, I'm liable to expire on the spot."

Fuck, she kept surprising him. Roman laughed; the sound was harsh with need. "Can't have that."

"No, we can't." She nipped the spot where his neck met his shoulder and then her hand was around the base of him, guiding his cock inside her.

He fought to keep the stroke steady and not drive into her like a goddamn beast. She clenched around him, one leg looping around his waist to take him deeper yet. *Heaven.* There was no other word to describe her little whimpers and shakes that he could feel all the way to the base of his cock. Or for her hands sliding down his back to grab his ass and drive him the rest of the way into her. He tangled his fingers in her hair and kissed her hard. "You know what you want."

"I want you."

He pulled almost all the way out of her and she rose to meet his thrust, her body moving in perfect time with his. As if they'd done this a thousand times before.

It was good. Too damn good.

He pulled back enough to create a little distance between their bodies. "Touch yourself. I said I want to feel you come on my cock, and I meant it."

She didn't hesitate, one hand snaking between her thighs, her middle finger circling her clit. The sight of her seeking her own pleasure while they were still joined threatened to toss him headfirst over the edge. He thrust again, hard enough to make her breasts bounce with each stroke.

Once. Twice. A third time.

She came with a cry, her mouth opening in a perfect O and her pussy milking him. He had no choice but to follow her under. Roman grabbed her hips and fucked her, pursuing his own pleasure even as her orgasm went on and on. Pressure built in the small of his spine and his balls drew up as he came hard enough to see stars.

He managed to collapse next to her instead of on top of her, but only barely. They lay there several long minutes as their gasping breath settled into something resembling normal. Roman pulled her closer, driven by some desire he didn't have a name for, and kissed her again.

She shifted toward him and hooked her other leg around his waist. "God, I just came harder than I've come in living memory and I already want you again. Do you have some kind of aphrodisiac in your sweat?" She licked his throat. "I think you might."

He rolled onto his back, taking her with him so

she sprawled on his chest. "If I do, then you do, too." Sure enough, his cock was already stirring.

She squirmed against him, her smile conveying that she knew exactly how hot the move was. "Is it still a one-night stand if we keep having sex until we're both walking funny tomorrow?"

He opened his mouth, reconsidered and shut it. Telling her to stay as long as they were both on the island was premature in the extreme— and would interfere with his business here. He couldn't forget his purpose, not even for this beautiful creature staring at his mouth as if she wanted it all over her body again.

Business would wait until tomorrow.

Roman coasted a hand down her spine, bringing her more firmly against him. "It's still night, so the possibilities are endless."

"I like the way you think."

"Trust me, I'll give you reason to like a whole lot more than that."

Allie woke up to his mouth on her pussy. Again. In the few hours since they'd passed out after having sex again, he'd woken her up three— *three*—times like that, and proceeded to ravish her until her promise that they'd both be walking funny today was definitely a reality rather than a possibility.

His big shoulders spread her legs wide and he

fucked her with his tongue, his low growls just as hot as his actions. She slid her fingers through his hair without opening her eyes. "Yes. Right there. Keep doing that." He zeroed in on her clit, mimicking the movements she'd made when she touched herself and pushing her to the edge yet again.

She didn't stand a chance of holding out.

She came with a cry, back bowing and her hands clenching him to her to prolong the pleasure as if she was totally and completely wanton. Maybe she was. She certainly had played the part that night, with no thought to what he'd think of her words or actions because this was only temporary. They were strangers, which was freeing in a way she'd never anticipated. It didn't mean she'd ever do anything like this again, but she was going to enjoy every single second of her time with her Adonis before dawn came.

He left her for several precious moments, but then he was back on the bed, flipping her onto her stomach and drawing her hips up. The position left her exposed, but she loved every second of it, especially when he stroked her between her thighs and then his cock replaced his fingers.

He pushed into her with a smooth move, sheathing himself to the hilt. And then he began to move, thrusting roughly into her and then withdrawing, only to begin again. Allie gripped the comforter and shoved back to meet him, until the only sound in the villas was the smack of flesh against flesh and their ragged breathing. She tried to hold out, tried to keep from being overwhelmed with the pleasure, but he did something with his hips that hit a spot deep inside her, and her orgasm crested in a devastating wave. She cried out, distantly aware of him fucking her harder until he, too, came with a curse.

He dropped to the side and guided her down with him so that they lay spooning with him still inside her. He kissed the back of her neck and palmed her breasts. "Morning."

"Mmm. And a good one at that." She still hadn't opened her eyes, but as one of his hands trailed down to her clit, she laughed hoarsely. "You're insatiable."

"Only with you." He kept up those slow kisses to the nape of her neck. "You make me crazy. I just came and I want you again already." He cupped her pussy, the possessive move making her moan.

But then she opened her eyes and realized how light it was outside. Allie froze. "What time is it?" If Becka woke up and realized she'd never come back last night, she'd be worried. Allie was reliable and dependable, and she most certainly didn't stay out all night while having amazing sex with a stranger. As beyond amazing as it'd been, she hadn't stopped to consider that her friend might think she was hurt or that something bad had happened.

He picked up on her tension and removed his hand. "What's wrong?"

"I have to go." She rolled out of his arms, her body crying out at the loss of warmth, but if Becka wasn't already awake, Allie had to make sure she got back to the villa before that happened. If she *was*, then Allie had some explaining to do.

Either way, she couldn't stay there.

He sat up and watched her scramble for her dress, a frown marring his handsome face. "I know we joked about it being a one-night stand, but that doesn't mean you have to bolt the second the sun comes up. I thought we could have breakfast before you left."

It sounded just as wonderful and perfect as things had been since she'd taken his hand and embarked on this wild adventure.

Unfortunately, reality was calling—or as close to reality as a person got on West Island.

But she didn't like the look on his face—as if she'd somehow hurt him—so she paused. "I would love that, but my friend is back at our villa, and if she wakes up and finds me gone, she's going to think that I walked off the path and broke my leg or something and sound the alarm. I don't have an easy way to get ahold of her, so I have to go make sure she's not forming a search party."

His frown cleared. "I understand." He got out of bed and pulled on his shorts. "I'll give you a ride back."

She started to tell him she didn't need that, but the truth was she did. It was one thing to take his cart because she'd changed her mind about being with him and didn't want to walk the paths alone at night. It was another to want to skip a potentially awkward morning-after conversation. She was an adult. She could handle it.

She hoped. "Thanks. That would be helpful."

He threw on his shirt but didn't bother buttoning it. It gave him the look of a... She didn't even know, but she liked it. A lot. *Down, girl.* She found her shoes and followed him out to the golf cart.

Allie was so tense as she sat next to him, she was surprised she didn't jostle right out of the seat when he put the cart into gear, but he reached over and took her hand, interlacing their fingers as if they held hands all the time. She relaxed, muscle by muscle, but her nerves didn't calm. "I don't do that normally—any of it."

"You don't have to explain yourself to me." He squeezed her hand. "I had a good time last night."

"Me...too." She studied his profile. Adonis, indeed. "A really good time."

He shot her a look as he took a turn onto a path marked with her villa number. "I'm in danger of being pushy, but I'd like to have a repeat—or several. I'm here on business, but my nights are yours if you're interested."

Her breath caught in her throat, though she couldn't say why. To spend her days with Becka doing all the activities they had planned and her nights with her Adonis... That truly would be paradise. She licked her lips. "I...I'd like that."

He grinned and pulled to a stop where the cart path ended and the walking path began. "In that case, would you gift a poor man with your name? You'll always be Aphrodite to me, but I'd like to know the true identity of the woman I plan to have coming countless times in the next few days."

She blushed and then called herself an idiot for blushing. "I'm Allie."

He went so still, he might as well have turned into a statue. Those hazel eyes focused on her with unsettling intensity. "Allie? Allie *Landers*?"

She jerked her hand back, her heart beating for a reason that had nothing to do with desire. "How do you know my last name?"

He laughed, but not like anything was funny. "This is so fucked."

"What are you talking about?"

Gone was the devilishly charming Adonis

who'd seduced her with little effort last night, replaced by a cold man she didn't recognize. "Roman Bassani."

She knew that name. She *knew* that name. Allie scrambled out of the cart and took several steps back, though he made no move to touch her again. "The guy who keeps hounding me? What the hell are you doing *here*?"

His smile was as cold as any she'd seen. "I'm here to convince you to sell your business."

CHAPTER FIVE

ROMAN WATCHED THE metaphorical shit hit the fan in slow motion. He looked at his Aphrodite—at *Allie Landers*—in disbelief. The horror in her expression, the way she took a step back and her body language closed down. Gone was the flirty siren he'd just had in his bed, replaced by a woman who didn't trust him as far as she could throw him.

Still, he tried to salvage it. "I can explain."

"Explain how you hunted me down to West Island and seduced me." She shook her head, blond hair flying. "Nope. Absolutely not. You pulled one over on me. Good job. Way to go. Points for being totally and completely unexpected. You don't get to stand there and tell me you can explain, because this is beyond explanation."

"I didn't know you were…you." He scrubbed his hands over his face. "I'm fucking this up."

"You think?" She took another step back.

"Your reputation might be shady, but I never expected *this*."

He started to explain why he thought she couldn't possibly be Allie Landers, but cut the words off before they reached the air between them. Telling her that her glorious curves didn't fit in a specialized gym was both shitty and wrong, and he'd have realized that he shouldn't assume a single goddamn thing if he'd stopped thinking with his cock long enough to function. *There has to be a way to salvage this.* "I don't see why this has to change anything."

Her blue eyes went wide. "You don't think this needs to change anything." She drew herself up to her full height, somewhere close to six feet. "You're out of your goddamn mind. Get out of here. I never want to see you again."

"Like hell I will." He hadn't wanted to do it like this. In fact, he'd crafted several well-thought-out arguments about how she needed to listen to his investment proposal. All of that flew right out the window in the face of his frustration. "You're going to lose it all if you don't stop being so fucking stubborn and let my investor help you."

She looked at him like she'd never seen him before. "Wanting to preserve what I worked so hard to create isn't stubbornness—and not wanting to sell it out to someone like *you* doesn't make me an idiot." She motioned at him.

"Someone like me." She'd made it sound like an insult, and maybe it was. Roman played dirty. He'd never had any qualms about that truth. He still wouldn't have tried to seduce Allie into seeing things his way—but he would have done everything else under the sun. He still would.

But her obvious disdain stung. He laughed harshly. "Someone like me," he repeated. "Honey, look in the mirror. There's only one reason Transcend is going under, and it's not me. I'm just trying to save it."

Her lips twisted. "How noble of you. Well, you can take your apparent white-knight complex and shove it up your ass." She spun around and marched down the path toward her villa, her middle finger in the air.

Stubborn, frustrating woman.

Admittedly, he could have played that better. Roman pinched the bridge of his nose for a long moment and then turned the cart around and headed back for his place. If he could just tell her *who* his investor was…

Impossible. He'd signed a nondisclosure, which his investor had insisted on. Even if he wanted to tell Allie the details of what his client had planned for her gym and shelter, he couldn't. Judging by her reaction, it wouldn't have mattered anyway. She would have called him a liar and told him he was full of shit.

He'd miscalculated. It wouldn't have changed the reaction he'd had to seeing Allie in person—he didn't think anything could have altered that—but he'd have kept control enough not to try to seduce her.

Fool. He could almost hear his old man's voice as if the bastard sat next to him. *Took the easy way and look what happened—exactly what always happens. Failure.*

Roman shut that shit down. He didn't have time to wallow in shame for fucking up. He had to figure out a way around it. As tempting as it was to follow her back to her villa and continue the argument until she saw things his way, it wouldn't do anything but make her dig in her heels further. Allie had proved herself to be as stubborn as the day was long. For some reason, she was resistant to investors.

He needed to figure out why. It was the only way to get around her issues.

He took a shower and headed into the main lodge. It was the only place to get a call out on the island or to use anything resembling the internet. It took some convincing to get the woman on staff to give him access to the tiny business center, but he managed.

Roman sat down while the computer hissed and spit in the old-school dial-up sounds. He shook his head. Apparently paradise didn't like modern technology. Go figure. He considered his best options and dialed Aaron Livingston. It was late enough in the morning that the man should be at the office.

Sure enough, he answered on the fourth ring. "Aaron Livingston."

"Aaron, Roman here."

"Hey, Roman, it's been a while. What can I do for you?"

Roman hadn't spent much time out and about since the fiasco with Gideon and Lucy, and as a result, his social life had suffered a bit. He hadn't cared—it was a nice change of pace—but he hoped it wouldn't work against him now that he needed a favor. "I was hoping you could do a bit of a background check on a company I'm considering investing in. I've done the run-of-the-mill one, but the owner is being difficult and I need to know why."

"You mean they weren't down on their knees in awe at your greatness?" Aaron's amusement filtered through the line. "Color me shocked."

"You don't have to rub it in. I missed a step, and I need to figure out where."

Aaron laughed. "You'll have to give me a few minutes to get over my surprise that the vaunted Roman Bassani isn't perfect."

"Asshole."

"Without a doubt." Another laugh. "Give me

the business name and I'll see what I can do. It might take me a few days, but I'll find the information you need."

"Thanks, man. I appreciate it."

"Yeah, well, I *am* charging you."

He grinned. "I wouldn't expect anything different." He hung up after Aaron told him to expect the information via email. It wasn't ideal, but he could wait through the long dial-up time to get it if that meant he had a leg to stand on with Allie.

Allie.

Roman sat back and scrubbed his hands over his face. It was time to deal with the fact that he'd fucked up. He might have fucked up badly enough that this account was lost...

No.

Damn it, *no*.

She was doing good work, but that good work could be increased exponentially if she allowed his client to invest and do the equivalent of franchising Transcend. It was a brilliant business model—or it would be if she moved a few things around.

Except she hadn't taken his meetings or returned his calls, and now she was doubly determined to stay the hell away from him. *Fuck me.* He had to fix this, to do something to get her to stop long enough to listen to what he had to say.

She was stubborn. She'd more than proved

that. Well, it was too damn bad, because he could be a stubborn bastard, too.

Roman checked his email, verified that the sky wasn't falling back in New York and logged off. It was time to figure out a game plan to get moving again. They were trapped on this damn island together for the next six days, and he'd be damned before he let this opportunity pass because of one mistake.

Though he'd be lying if he considered last night a mistake. He should have gotten her name immediately, but if he had, the night wouldn't have happened. Having Allie in his bed... He stomped down on his body's reaction to the memories that rolled through him, one after another. Her taste on his tongue. The feel of her generous hips in his hands. Her pussy clenching around his cock. The little smirk she gave him when she knew her saucy attitude was flat-out doing it for Roman.

He'd give his left hand for a repeat. *Get your priorities in order, asshole. She might be hotter than sin and amazing in bed and funny as fuck, but she's still business.*

Roman couldn't afford to forget that—or let the lines blur.

"Roman Bassani followed you *here*?"

Allie adjusted her balance on the paddleboard and dipped her paddle into the water. "I already said that." She glared at the gorgeous water. Stupid paradise, making *her* stupid. She knew better than to go home with a man whose name she didn't even know. *You didn't go home with him, because neither of you are home right now.*

Not helping.

"I just… That's ballsy. Even for Roman."

She twisted so fast, she almost fell off the damn board. "You say his name like you know him." Something resembling jealousy curled thorny vines through her stomach. She had no right to the feeling, and it made no rational sense, so she ignored it.

"Well…I kind of do." Becka shrugged. She wore a bikini so tiny, it must have taken an act of God to keep it in place. It was a bright neon green that managed to complement her equally bright blue hair. "Or we have one degree of separation, but I've met him once, I think. He was a friend of my sister—*is* a friend of my sister." She shook her head. "You know the story, but yeah, he's really good friends with her boyfriend and so they all hang out sometimes now. But I know him by reputation, at least, and he's the best at what he does."

That was part of the problem—Allie wasn't one hundred percent sure what he *did* do. He'd contacted her about investing in Transcend, but it quickly became clear he was a middleman for someone else and… She didn't know. Trusting an investor was difficult enough without them hiding behind a third party. That extra distance didn't bode well for her being able to maintain control of the gym and shelter if she signed on the dotted line. She'd come to West Island to escape real life for a little bit, and it'd followed her here despite her best efforts.

And then she'd slept with it.

She frowned. *Way to make the metaphor weird, Allie.* "It doesn't matter. It was a mistake and I'm going to enjoy the rest of my damn vacation without worrying about him." She was lying through her teeth, but she sent a look at her best friend, daring Becka to call her on it.

Becka dipped her paddle into the water, moving farther away from the beach. "I don't know, Allie. He's one sexy golden god of a man. What would it hurt to bang him like a conga drum while you're down here and go back to hating him when you get home?"

"He's *Roman Bassani.* He's the enemy. I can't just separate things like he apparently can." Though he'd been just as shocked at her identity as she was at his. Allie knew that for a fact. The man might be a good actor, but no one was *that* good. She didn't believe for a second that he'd tried to manipulate her through sex, but that didn't mean she was about to roll over and offer herself and everything she'd worked so hard for to him just because he was beautiful and had an amazing cock and—

Not helping.

"What would a little hot and smoking sex hurt?"

She splashed water at Becka. "It wouldn't *hurt*, but the man already doesn't take me seriously. If he thinks he can seduce me into seeing things his way, who's to say he won't do exactly that?"

Becka sighed. "You're right. I know you're right. It's just so… This place. It makes everything sexier and less complicated, and even though vodka and I broke up, vodka would most definitely agree that it's a good idea."

"Then it's a good thing you and vodka broke up." They reached the mouth of their little bay and paused, letting the paddleboards shift with the water. She lay back on the board and closed her eyes, willing the sun to soak in and chase away her tension. "It's not fair. I am so damn furious that he pulled this shit, but my body hasn't got the memo. He's just so hot. It makes me crazy." She was pretty sure she had the self-control to keep her hands off him going forward, but Allie wasn't all that eager to put it to the test.

"Yes…yes, he is."

There was something in her friend's tone that made her open her eyes. Allie shot up to a sitting position. "Tell me that the sun has gone to my head and I'm hallucinating."

"If you are, we're sharing the view." Becka adjusted her kneeling position like she was going to war. "I can distract him if you want to make a break for it."

That ugly jealousy rose again, even though there'd been nothing resembling insinuation in her friend's tone. Anyway, Allie had *just* said that she wanted nothing to do with him. She couldn't have it both ways. And Becka was... Becka was a force of nature. *Stop that right this second. She's your friend, and he's not anything to you.*

The "he" in question rowed his kayak toward them in smooth movements that made the muscles in his shoulders and chest flex—kind of like they had when he was hovering over her and thrusting...

Her face flamed, and she shook out her hair, doing her best to pretend it was just the external heat and not his effect on her. When Roman got close enough for her to see his face clearly, she went still. He wasn't looking at Becka at all. His attention had focused on Allie like a laser beam, and he cut through the water, effortlessly back paddling to coast to a stop next to her paddleboard. "Allie."

"I'm not sure of the exact laws in this place, but I'm pretty sure they frown on stalking."

His lips quirked. "It's a small island. We're bound to run into each other."

How could he sit there so calm and collected while she fought between the desire to tip his damn kayak and to jump him where he sat? She steadied her grip on her paddle and fought for control. It was easier—so much easier—to be angry than it was to deal with the conflicting emotions inside her. "Is that what you call your kayaking past our villa—again?"

His grin was quick and unrepentant. "The view isn't as good this time." She sputtered, but he didn't give her a chance to reply, turning instead to look at Becka. "I know you."

"Not really. But you know my sister—Lucy Baudin."

He flinched—actually *flinched*—though he covered it up quickly enough that Allie wouldn't have noticed it if she wasn't watching him so closely. Becka had said her sister and Roman were friends, but it appeared to be more complicated than that. Allie filed that away, and irritation rose all over again. "We're trying to have a relaxing time, and you're ruining it."

Roman turned the force of his attention onto her again. His wearing sunglasses should have diluted the effect, but she swore she could feel his gaze dragging over her, taking in her high-waisted vintage swimsuit. It was a flirty black with pink polka dots, and she knew she looked damn good in it. From the way his grip tightened on his paddle, he agreed.

A strange sense of power rolled through her. He wanted her just as much as she wanted him. She'd known that, of course, but the shock of his true identity had twisted everything up in her head. Roman might be considering trying to seduce her into submission, but… What if she turned the tables on him?

Or maybe you want any excuse to get into bed with him again.

She ignored the internal voice and leaned forward, giving him a good view of the excellent cleavage the underwire top created. A muscle ticked in his jaw, and she reveled in the power for a breath before reason kicked back in. "Get lost, Roman. You don't have anything to say to me that I want to hear."

"We both know that's not true." His wicked grin widened, leaving no illusions to what he meant.

Her irritation flickered hotter. He was sitting there, the smug bastard, and thinking he had her number just because he'd made her come more times last night than she'd thought physically possible. Thinking he could railroad her into doing what he wanted.

Well, fuck that.

Allie lifted her chin. "I don't know anything of the sort. It was a forgettable experience across the board." She jerked her chin at Becka, who watched them with jaw dropped. "Let's go. Something stinks out here."

CHAPTER SIX

ROMAN SPENT THE rest of the day considering his game plan. Cornering Allie was all well and good, but from the look she'd given him before she paddled away early, if she thought he was trying to talk business, she'd cut him off at the knees. *Misplayed the hell out of this.*

There was no use bitching about it. The ideal situation was long gone, so he had to work with what he had.

What he had was smoking-hot chemistry with Allie Landers. Seeing her in that cocktease of a swimsuit with her hair in beach waves around her shoulders hadn't done a damn thing to help remind him why he couldn't have her.

He decided to give her until tomorrow—or, rather, to give *himself* until tomorrow—to figure it out. Rushing this wasn't going to accomplish the end he wanted.

He checked his email, more to distract himself

than because he thought there'd be any information yet. There wasn't even a single fire for him to put out. Roman ran his hand through his hair. Paradise was all well and good in theory, but it was fucking boring here by himself.

On a whim, he made his way to the patio where sunset yoga would be held—and stopped short at the sight of Allie in a pair of yoga pants and a tank top that seemed to have too many straps but showed off her body to perfection. As he watched, she pulled her hair back into a ponytail and unrolled a mat.

The instructor—a tiny woman with dark eyes, curly hair and a wide smile—caught sight of him. "The mats are against the wall. Pick a place that feels best for you, but we do prefer to have classes in a single line when there's a small number of people."

Allie turned and her eyebrows shot up, then lowered just as fast. "What are you doing here?"

"Yoga." There was no backing out now, even if he wasn't going to get the relaxation he'd craved. He'd wanted to get time with Allie to talk, but this wasn't what Roman had in mind. He grabbed one of the mats and flung it out with a snap a decent distance from hers. On her other side, Becka looked between them as if she wasn't sure how she was supposed to react.

The instructor was all smiles and gentle hands

as she picked up his mat and scooted it until it was only a few inches from Allie's. "Yoga is meant to be experienced as a group. We like to keep it intimate here—which we can't do if someone is creating distance." Once she was satisfied he'd obey, she moved to the front of their line and started her intro.

Roman tried to do yoga a few times a week. He spent too much time sitting behind a desk, and he preferred boxing as his outlet—both activities wreaked havoc on his joints. Yoga helped, and it settled his racing mind like little else, he found.

Today, there was no settling to be had.

He had too much awareness of Allie next to him, her body flowing through the positions effortlessly, her breathing deep and even. *She* didn't seem the least bit bothered to have him so close. It aggravated him in a way it shouldn't have, but he wanted to force her to acknowledge that he was *right there*.

"Roman, you seem distracted." The instructor— he couldn't remember her name, but it was something like Tiffany or Tracy—stopped next to him, using a light touch to adjust his Warrior I stance. "Focus on your breathing. Inhale deeply." She demonstrated, exhaling slowly through her nose in an audible sound. He followed suit, and she nodded. "Exhale your thoughts. Let your breath center you. You gave yourself this time today. Don't waste it."

He tried. Fuck, he tried. But each inhale brought a faint strain of Allie's lavender scent, and when she turned to face the side of the patio, he found himself captivated by the faint sheen of sweat on her golden skin.

It was too much.

With his being so goddamn in tune with his body, there was no fighting the threatening cock-stand. Roman turned on his heel and stalked away, into the main building. He needed distance from that woman, but fuck if it helped. Her scent was in his system, her body a siren call he had no business hearing. She didn't want him—not now that she knew who he was.

He shouldn't want her, either.

But he did.

Roman considered heading straight back to his villa, but the thought of being alone right now only increased his agitation. *This was a mistake.* Which part was the biggest mistake was up for grabs, but he was considering chalking the entire situation up as a loss.

With nothing left to do, he walked into the bar. It was a small space—no more than a serving counter with a handful of lounge chairs facing the ocean—as everything on the island was. He motioned to the bartender. "I need two shots of whiskey, and a double seven and seven."

The man's eyebrows rose. "Sure thing. You've

got the run of the place, so post up wherever you like." He turned back to select two bottles from the wall behind him.

Roman didn't want to sit, but standing there and hovering while the guy made his drinks wasn't going to win him any goodwill. He had enough people pissed at him currently, so he strode to the middle lounger and dropped into it.

Lazy streaks of color teased the darkening blue of the sky, the first sign of day giving way to night. Roman welcomed the change even as he dreaded what it meant. Another day down. Another night closer to failure.

It might not be the end of the world if he didn't secure Allie's cooperation in franchising her gym model, but her gym *would* go under. He'd seen the financials. She couldn't keep it afloat much longer, and it'd be a goddamn tragedy to see it fail. He knew she didn't look at it that way, but if she'd stop fucking *reacting* and listen to what he had to say, she might see things differently.

Right. Because I've been the very essence of calm and collected.

Her rejection stung. He wasn't about to lie and say it didn't. It sure as hell did. She hadn't just rejected the professional persona he displayed for work—she'd rejected *him*. The sex changed things, for better or worse. *Looking like for the worst at the moment.*

The bartender brought his shots over and lined them up, quickly followed by his drink. Alcohol wasn't the best choice—not when he needed to be sharp and fully present—but he wasn't going to be around Allie tonight, and the rest of the island could sink into the sea for all he cared. Roman downed one shot and then the second. The fiery burn of whiskey did nothing to chase away his... He didn't even know what the fuck to call what he was feeling. It wasn't pleasant—that was all that mattered.

Women's voices carried over the beach, and he tensed. Before she walked around the corner, Roman already recognized Allie's voice. She stopped short when she saw him, but Becka rolled her eyes and gave her friend a small shove. "Enough, already. I get it—he's a jerk. I won't even argue with you." She winked at Roman, not looking the least bit repentant. "But I want a drink, and this is the quickest way to get what I want." She gave a brilliant smile to someone behind Roman. "Hey, gorgeous. Can we get something fruity and alcoholic?"

"Sure thing, ma'am."

Becka launched into how horrified she was to be called "ma'am" while she walked to the bar, but Allie stopped at the foot of Roman's lounger. "You ran off pretty unexpectedly."

He gave her body a slow caress with his gaze,

from her bright pink painted toes to her yoga pants to the tank top that offered her breasts up to perfection. "I was preoccupied."

She inhaled sharply, and he didn't miss the way her nipples pebbled against the fabric of her shirt. "Don't play games with me. It happened. We're done. End of story. Stop bringing it up."

"I didn't bring it up." He climbed to his feet slowly and then closed the distance between them. "A word."

"Excuse me?"

"We need to have a goddamn conversation, so get your panties out of a twist long enough to un-stopper your ears and hear what I have to say." He grabbed her hand and towed her into the grow-ing shadows beneath the palm trees framing the walkway to the beach. Roman didn't stop until they were out of sight of the bar and far enough away that Becka's flirting with the bartender was barely audible. Only then did he release Allie and turn to face her. "Now, where were we?"

Allie was so furious, she could barely put two words together. "You don't get to just decide that we're having a conversation and haul me out here to do it."

"If I was going to *haul* you anywhere, it'd be over my shoulder."

Her body clenched at the thought of him doing

exactly that, but she fought her reaction back. "You are insufferable. Do you know when the last time I had a vacation was? Ten goddamn years ago when I was still in freaking high school and on spring break. Ten. *Years.* Becka had to twist my arm to get me here, but I was enjoying myself—"

"I know *exactly* how thoroughly you were enjoying yourself."

She ignored that because if she tried to deny it, she'd be a red-faced liar. "That changes nothing. The point is that I'm *not* enjoying myself now, and the only one to blame for that is *you.*" She went to push him back a step, but her hands had a will of their own. They stayed on his chest, and she sucked in a breath at how warm his skin was. The man might be a corporate suit, but he looked perfectly at home in his shorts without a shirt on here in the growing darkness near the beach. It was almost enough to forget all the reasons she never wanted to see him again.

Allie stepped closer and lowered her voice. "Nothing you say can make me believe you're anything but a goddamn shark."

"Who said I'm trying to convince you of anything?" The words brushed her mouth as he leaned down, just a little. "I *am* a shark, Allie. I've never pretended to be anything else."

She started to call him a liar, but he was telling the truth. He hadn't tried to seduce her with sweet words to get her into his bed—he'd offered her exactly what she wanted in as many words. Black-and-white. Simple.

It wasn't simple at all.

"I despise you."

"You want me." His hands rested lightly on her hips. "It tears you up inside that you crave my cock, but you can't fight it no matter how hard you try." He backed her up, step by slow step, until she bumped a tree. Roman kept coming, the side of his face brushing hers. "Did you think about how good it'd feel to have my fingers sliding into these yoga pants?"

"No."

"Who's the liar now, Allie?" His lips caressed her earlobe. "I'd love a private yoga session. Just us. No friends, no instructors, no clothes. How long do you think we'd last before I was on my back and you were riding my cock?"

She couldn't breathe. Her skin felt too tight, as if it were several sizes too small, and her core pulsed in time with her racing heart. "I would never—"

"No, Allie. No more lies between us. You're pissed that I'm here—I get that—and you're even more pissed that you want me. Trust me, I know the feeling. I was never supposed to fuck you, and if I'd known who you were..."

She leaned back enough to look at his face—

or what she could see of it in the darkness. "If you'd known who I was, you wouldn't have gone there with me."

Roman cursed. "Even if I'd known your name, that wouldn't have stopped me from wanting you. Needing you."

She stroked her hands down his chest to the waistband of his shorts. "Do you need me now?"

"I never stopped."

This was the worst idea. She needed her head clear, and it was nothing but muddled around Roman. He was too big, too beautiful, too over-powering. Even now, she leaned forward, the few inches between them too much distance. He let her, his hands on her hips branding her—but not trying to guide her. Allie inhaled deeply. "Do you drug your cologne? Because, seriously, how am I supposed to think straight when you smell so good?"

He chuckled. "I'm not wearing any."

He was gorgeous and a god in the bedroom, and he had to smell good naturally. Because of course. "I don't like you."

"You don't know me."

She could argue that, but it didn't feel com-pletely accurate. Allie traced the waistband of his shorts with her fingers. She shouldn't...but she was going to. She unbuttoned his shorts and slipped her hand in to grip his cock. "I don't have to know you—I know this."

"You're playing with fire."

"Maybe." Definitely. If she was smart, she'd release him, walk away and spend the rest of her vacation in as close to bliss as she could get, throwing herself into relaxation before she had to go back to reality. She stroked him again, liking the way his body went tense but his hands stayed still on her hips.

As if he was waiting for permission.

The realization sent a thrill through her. She kept stroking his cock, teasing him. "Did you really think it would be that easy?"

"What would?" He spoke through gritted teeth, and her body gave another thrill of pleasure.

"Getting your way." She squeezed him around the base and nudged his pants down a little farther so she could cup his balls with her free hand. "You thought you'd show up here, interrupt my vacation and what? I'd fall all over myself to give you exactly what you wanted?"

Roman released one of her hips and braced his hand on the tree behind her. The move brought him closer to her, but not so close that he impeded her movements. She stroked him harder as he slid his cheek against hers, his breathing hitching with every downstroke. He nipped her earlobe. "Isn't that exactly what happened last night?"

She glared and gave his balls a squeeze that was just shy of vicious. "You're awfully cocky for someone who's got their nether bits in my hands."

"They're very capable hands." He shifted to press butterfly kisses along her jaw and down her neck even as his hand on her hip squeezed her. "Don't stop."

"I should." She didn't. "I should stop right now and leave you with a wicked case of blue balls." Why was her breath coming as harshly as his? He'd barely touched her, but having his cock in her hands and him so close… Intoxicating. There was no other word for it.

Roman gave her collarbone an openmouthed kiss and dragged his hand up her side to palm her breast. "I'll just go back to my villa and jack myself off thinking of your sweet pussy. Not as good as the real thing—nothing is—but you gave me more than enough inspiration to get the job done." He tugged the strap of her tank top off her shoulder. It was one of those things with a built-in bra, so the motion freed her breast. He repeated the move with the other side, and she shivered as the breeze coming in off the water teased her nipples. "Beautiful," Roman murmured.

"You go overboard with the compliments." She kept up her leisurely stroking. It was like the rest of the world ceased to exist outside their little sphere. It was just her and Roman, driving each other crazy.

"I give credit where credit is due." He bent and sucked one nipple into his mouth. The position meant she had to let go of his cock, which she did with reluctance. He cupped her through her yoga pants, the coolness of the tree against her back only highlighting how warm his body was. "If I slipped my hand in here, would I find you wet and wanting? I think so." He traced a single finger up the seam of the pants—right over her clit. "I think having my cock in your hands turned you on as much as the fact that we're ten yards away from the bar and anyone coming up from the beach will get the show of their life."

She pushed back against him even as her hips rolled into his touch. "That's not true."

"Liar." She felt more than heard the word as his breath caressed her neck. "You get off on this as much as I do." Another stroke through the fabric. "Would you take my cock right here, right now?"

She started to say yes, but common sense reared its ugly head. "I'm not fucking you without a condom."

"Mmm." He kissed her neck. "I know." Roman pulled her pants down in a swift movement. She started to protest, but he went to his knees in front of her and yanked her foot free. *Oh.* He looped one leg over his shoulder and she caught the glimpse of white teeth when he grinned. "Have a little faith, Allie. I'm not a complete monster." And then his mouth was on her pussy and she didn't have the breath to argue.

CHAPTER SEVEN

ALLIE FORGOT ALL the reasons she wanted nothing to do with Roman under the slow slide of his tongue. He tasted her pussy as if he'd been years without it and wanted to imprint every last detail on his memory. She bit back a cry and covered her mouth with one hand even as her other laced through his hair and pressed his face closer to her.

His dark chuckle vibrated over her clit, nearly sending her to outer space. What was he *doing* to her? She didn't act like this. She didn't screw strangers, and she definitely didn't let a man she was pretty sure she didn't like give her oral while in clear view of anyone who happened by.

He pushed two fingers into her and zeroed in on her clit, sucking and then flicking it with his tongue in a rhythm she couldn't have fought even if she wanted to. His fingers deep inside her circled that sensitive spot and he mirrored the movement with his tongue, driving her ruthlessly over the edge. Her hand muffled her cry, but only barely. Allie slumped against the tree and watched him press his forehead to her stomach as if trying to get control of himself.

As if fighting not to rise and drive that glorious cock into her right then.

Finally, he helped her get her foot back into her yoga pants and stepped back while she righted her clothing. Roman didn't speak, didn't look at her, and she couldn't help the dip of disappointment deep in her stomach.

Allie took a fortifying breath and turned for the bar. She needed a drink and to get the hell out of there. She could smell him on her skin, and between that and the orgasm, she was having a hard time remembering why Roman was off-limits.

So off-limits that I just had his mouth all over me.

She managed one step before a hand closed around her arm. Allie looked back, waiting to see what he'd do. Roman finally cursed and released her. "We need to talk, Allie. Actually talk."

Disappointment warred with righteous anger. "Wrong. As I've said half a dozen times already— I am on vacation." Her orgasm-induced high brought more words. "On the other hand, if you want this." She motioned to herself. "Then that's something we can negotiate." At the look on Roman's face, Allie almost took the offer back.

He stepped closer. "You want to separate business and pleasure."

"Business and pleasure should always be separate." She lifted her chin, half-amazed at how brazen she was being, but it wasn't as if she had anything to lose. Roman wasn't going to give up—the limited interactions she'd had with him up to this point reinforced that belief—and she also wasn't going to back down. They could either blow off some steam here on the island before they got back to her dodging his calls and his trying to buy her business out from under her, or they could go their separate ways now.

There was no happy medium. Not for them.

His gaze dropped to her mouth. "I can't promise that. The timeline is too tight and—"

"I don't want to hear it," she cut in. "If you can't promise you won't talk about business, then don't talk at all."

That delicious muscle in his jaw ticked. "You make it sound so simple."

"It is. It's exactly that simple."

Roman stared at her long enough that she had to fight not to squirm. He smiled, the expression doing nothing to quell the urge. She crossed her arms over her chest. "What?"

"I don't have to make any deals with you, Allie."

Again, disappointment tried to take over. She

fought it back down, but she was less successful this time. She had to make a conscious effort not to let her shoulders dip or her spine bend. "And why's that?"

"Because you want me as much as I want you." He traced a single finger down her throat and over her sternum. "You want me so badly, if I crooked my finger, you'd be back at my villa, naked and coming on my cock. You say you'll draw the line in the sand, and that's fine, but you'll be fighting yourself more than you'll be fighting me to keep from crossing it."

Her growing anger was almost a welcome relief. Allie knew how to be angry. She didn't let it control her, but most of her successes in life could be chalked up to doing things out of spite. A trailer trash girl from upstate New York couldn't go to college? Like hell she couldn't—and she'd get the majority of it paid for while she was in the process with volleyball scholarships. Having a forward-thinking women's-only gym that paired with a women's shelter was unconventional? Sure, it was. But that wasn't going to stop her from going for it full throttle.

Roman thought he could sit back, kick up his heels and let the lure of his cock draw her in after she'd laid out her terms?

Not fucking likely.

She pushed his hand away from her. "You're wrong."

"Am I?"

She wanted to smack that smug look off his face, but that wasn't how she operated. She stepped back and then stepped back again. "The terms are what they are. If you can't respect that, stay the hell away from me."

He blinked, as if he hadn't expected her response. "Allie—"

"No, you will not 'Allie' me as if I'm being irrational. I want you. We both know it. What *you* don't seem to be able to wrap your brain around is that while you might be ruled by your cock, *I* am more than capable of making decisions that aren't based in sex." She forced herself to turn around and walk away from him. "If you change your mind, you know where to find me."

She didn't give him a chance to respond before she picked up her pace and made her way back into the lantern light now illuminating the bar area. Becka turned away from the handsome bartender and raised her eyebrows. "You look like you've been up to no good."

"I have no idea what you're talking about." She took the bar stool next to her friend and downed the tequila shot waiting for her without hesitation.

"That was mine," Becka said mildly.

"I'll get you the next one." She shook her head.

"What am I saying? They're included." She'd lost her damn mind. There was no other explanation for how she was acting—like a horny teenager who didn't care what was at stake as long as she got hers. Allie was better than that. She had to be.

The bartender poured them each another shot and set a fresh margarita in front of Allie. "Ring the bell if you need me."

"Sure thing, sweetie." Becka barely waited for him to walk out of eyesight before she swung around to face Allie. "Explain yourself. I didn't think you needed assistance, but I can't tell if you've been in a fistfight or fucking against a tree."

Allie's face flamed. "We didn't have sex."

"But you did *something* against a tree." She shook her head. "For a woman who says you despise that man, you are having a hell of a time keeping your hands off him."

She started to protest, but what was the point? Allie could chalk up the night before to her not knowing who he was, but she didn't have that excuse this time. She knew who Roman was and why he was here, and she'd still stuck her hand down his pants. "I get around him and my rational brain shuts off. It's like I have a lady Neanderthal in there, and she's decided she really likes the look of Roman and wants to bang his brains out and to hell with the consequences."

"This is a new thing for you." Becka downed her shot and set the glass on the bar with a faint clink. "It's disconcerting, huh? To have rational Allie who follows all the rules overrun by the hindbrain."

That was exactly it. She kept saying she didn't do things like this, but only because it was the truth. Back in New York, Allie never would have laid down the offer she'd just given Roman. She wouldn't have gone home with him in the first place. She glared at her tequila shot. "I think they pump something into the air on this island to make people act irrational."

"Or maybe…just maybe—" Becka nudged the shot into her hand "—it might *possibly* be that you've been wound so tightly for a seriously long time that the first situation that arose where no one was depending on you, you let yourself live a little. You don't have to play whipping girl about this, Allie. It's okay to want him."

But it *wasn't* okay.

She didn't know how to reconcile the person she was back home and the woman she was acting like here. "I'm not supposed to want him. Anyone but him."

"Ah." Becka nodded and took a long drink of the pink thing in front of her. "I don't have an easy answer for that. You going to his place tonight?"

"No." She might want him more than she had

a right to, but that didn't change the fact that she *didn't* want to talk business with him—or, rather, fight about business. If he couldn't agree to that bare minimum, then the pleasure wasn't worth the pain.

She just had to keep reminding herself of that.

Roman didn't sleep well. Every noise brought him fully awake, sure that Allie had changed her mind. He knew she wouldn't. She had drawn that line in the sand and she was stubborn enough not to cross it. He might have bullshit her yesterday, but he knew the truth.

The ball was in his court.

He woke early and attended the sunrise yoga class. There were a few people there he didn't recognize, but neither Allie nor Becka showed up. It was a relief to turn off his mind for a bit, but the feeling lasted until he walked into the tiny business center and went through the irritating process of checking his email.

Aaron had come through for him.

Roman stared at the document for a long time before he printed it. Even if he decided to take Allie up on her offer, he still had his eye on the prize for when they got back to New York. That meant he needed the deeper research so he could figure out how to play this. They were down to the wire.

It wasn't completely his fault, but that didn't change the bottom line.

He gathered the papers, double-checked to make sure the document hadn't downloaded on the computer and logged off. There was plenty of time to get his reading done and then figure out how he'd plan the rest of the day. Accidentally running into Allie might be entertaining as fuck, but it wasn't accomplishing anything. He had to figure out a better way to go about this.

I could take her up on the offer.

Roman hesitated in front of his cart. It seemed simple enough—leave business out of things. It meant passing up valuable opportunities to talk to her, but…it wasn't like Allie was talking to him at this point. She wasn't going to, either. She'd made that more than clear.

There was no goddamn reason not to say yes.

He turned around and headed back into the main building. The hostess smiled when she saw him coming. "Mr. Bassani, are you enjoying your stay?"

"Very much so." He was about to enjoy it a whole hell of a lot more. He stopped next to the desk she stood behind. "I was hoping you could help me with something."

"Of course." She smiled brightly, her brown eyes lighting up with the rest of her face. "Let me know what you need and I'll take care of it."

"I'd like to send a message to one of the other villas—villa six."

Her face fell. "Oh, I'm sorry. We do our best to create an isolated and relaxing atmosphere here. If guests choose to come into the lodge, that's one thing, but we don't seek them out unless they need something." And she clearly thought that whatever he wanted to send wouldn't be relaxing.

Roman put on his most charming smile. "It's just a little note. If they order dinner tonight, there would already be someone going out there. You can just include the message with the food."

Still she hesitated. "I'm not sure."

"If it makes you feel better, you can read the note. Just to ensure it's all on the up-and-up."

Another hesitation, shorter this time. "I suppose…" She passed over a thick piece of island stationery. Roman accepted the pen and scrawled a quick note. The hostess frowned. "That's it?"

"She'll know what I mean."

She smiled, obviously put at ease by the fact he hadn't written anything inappropriate. Roman could have corrected her assumption, but he needed Allie to get that note. *Passing notes. That's what I've been reduced to.*

It would be hours yet before he knew what *her* answer was—possibly longer if she decided to make him wait. The entire thing was beyond his control, and it irritated the fuck out of him.

What was he supposed to do with this? Roman was used to seeing what he wanted and going for it—and heaven help anyone who thought they could stand in the way.

He wanted his client happy, and the only way that would happen was acquiring the gym.

He wanted Allie, too.

Therein lay the issue—he couldn't have both. There might not be any sort of future with Allie, but there sure as fuck wasn't one if he kept pushing her. She'd made that more than clear.

If he stopped pushing her, they could relax into the insanely hot sex, but he'd have to let his plan for Transcend go. It might not be the end of the world, but Roman's career was built on the faith that he could provide exactly what he promised. He'd never met an obstacle he couldn't account for and overcome.

Until now.

He turned and strode out of the main building and to his cart, gripping the stack of papers. All the information he could come up with for Allie and her gym—something Roman should have done a long time ago. Oh, he'd done the basic background check and pulled the available financial statements he could get ahold of, but he hadn't dug deeper than that, even when she'd refused to meet him.

Stupid of him.

He didn't need to navel gaze for the rest of his goddamn life to know why he hadn't pushed as hard as he normally did. *The shelter.* He admired the hell out of what she was doing there, and he knew it was pretty damn likely that she had some kind of history that drove her to create a safe space like she had. Having a man try to bulldoze her might trigger shit that he'd have to be a monster to pull up.

He'd played softball with her.

Now that he'd met Allie, he was forced to reevaluate. She wasn't anything like he'd expected. She wasn't a wilting flower that would crumble at a sharp word. The woman had thorns, and she had no problem using them. Roman gripped the papers. The gloves were coming off. Now.

CHAPTER EIGHT

ALLIE BARELY WAITED for the man to leave their covered food before she yanked the lids off. "I'm starving." If she'd spent any time wondering if she'd be active enough while on vacation, she needn't have worried. Swimming and paddle-boarding had left a pleasant soreness in her muscles and an equally pleasant tiredness.

Also, she'd been ready to wade into the ocean and try to catch her own fish if dinner hadn't shown up when it did.

Becka laughed and bumped Allie with her hip. "They also brought vodka. Your priorities are suspect."

"Food always trumps vodka." She speared a glazed shrimp with her fork and then grabbed a chair. "I'm glad to see that you and vodka are back on speaking terms."

"We're taking it slow." Becka pulled up a second chair and sank into it. "My shoulders are kill-ing me. I obviously need to add more push-ups to my routine."

Allie laughed. "The girls will love that." Her friend had a reputation for being a brutal fitness instructor—a reputation she'd more than earned—and this would only cement it. One of the biggest draws Transcend offered was high-energy spin classes with combined exercises that worked the entire body. She reached for the pitcher of cucumber water in the middle of the table and froze. "What is that?"

Becka reacted first and snatched up the little folded note. She read it and frowned. "What the hell *is* it?" She turned it around, and Allie's heart skipped a beat.

Yes.

The word had been scrawled with a careless masculine hand, and even though it wasn't signed, she had no doubt who had written it. *He accepted my terms.* A flush spread over her skin, and even though she tried to fight it, Becka saw.

Because of course she did. She dropped the note and pointed a finger at Allie. "It's from Roman. You sly fox, I thought you were calling the whole thing off."

Allie pushed her food around the plate with her fork. "I told him if he could keep from badgering me about business—or even talking about it— then we could spend more time together."

"That was the tamest euphemism for banging your brains out that I've ever heard." Her friend slouched back into her chair and laughed. "Vacation has done wonders for your stress level. I told you so."

"The guy trying to convince me to sell the gym that I worked my entire adult life to get started and keep running followed me to another country to pitch his sale, and you call this trip a success."

Becka shrugged, completely unrepentant. "You took care of that by removing business from the equation. Now there's only the hot monkey sex to worry about, and I think you two have proved that you're more than capable of keeping your eye on the prize." She made an obscene gesture.

Allie spit out the sip of water she'd just taken. "Oh. My. God."

"Just calling it like I see it." Becka winked. "But seriously—if he's willing to shelve that big black mark against him, are you going for it?"

There was no reason to think he was telling the truth. He could be trying to pull a bait and switch to get her alone. But that didn't make sense. He could have found a different way. Roman had more than proved how capable he was in tracking her down. He had no reason to agree if he wasn't interested in exactly the same thing she was—sex.

Her body clenched at the thought. Allie set her fork down. "I think so."

"Woot!" Becka gave a little wiggle. "That's my girl. In that case, I'm bringing that delightful bartender, Luke, back here for some of said hot monkey sex."

She shot her friend a look. "You wouldn't, by chance, be throwing me at Roman so you can hook up with Luke?"

"Oh, please. We both know that I'm more than capable of finding a suitable place to get under that uniform if I have to." Becka sobered. "But I don't want to get him into trouble, so the villa is a better option." She held her straight face for all of two seconds. "What are you waiting for? Go! Get your…" Becka stopped short, her expression turning wicked. "He's stacked, isn't he? You can just tell by how he carries himself that the man is packing serious heat."

"*Becka.*" Allie laughed, which broke the tension that had been building from the moment she realized Roman had changed his mind. She sat back in her chair. "You did that on purpose."

"You're stressing, which is the opposite of what you're supposed to do here." Becka popped a strawberry into her mouth. "I helped."

"Yes, you did." She looked at the food, but her stomach was tied in too many knots to think about eating right now. Allie pushed back her chair and stood. "I guess I should…change?"

Becka picked through the food and added more to her plate. "You want my advice?"

"As if saying no would stop you from giving it to me." She snagged one of the bright red strawberries and took a bite.

"Wear that." Becka waved a fork at her.

Allie looked down at her muscle tank top and sleep shorts. "This is not sexy."

"Lose the bra and whatever you're wearing under the shorts." She grinned. "If he doesn't take you right there on the floor, I'll give you twenty bucks."

Allie walked across the warm sand to Roman's brightly lit villa. Soft music emerged, and though she couldn't quite place the lyrics, the lilting melody drew her in. She made her way up the porch stairs and stopped just outside the ring of light from the foremost lamp.

"You're teasing me."

She jumped and then silently cursed herself for jumping. Allie searched the spot where his voice had come from, only making him out of the shadows when he moved closer. "How long were you lurking there, waiting to make your grand entrance?"

"Would you believe me if I said I went for a swim to burn off some energy and just got back?"

She started to call his bluff, but he walked into the light and, sure enough, he wore wet swim trunks and his hair dripped tiny rivers down his shoulders and chest. It took more effort than it should have to drag her gaze to his face. "Swimming in the ocean at night is stupid."

"I survived." He held out his hand, as imperious as a king. "Come here."

Allie had never been one to make an entrance, but she found herself wanting to prove Becka right. She threw her shoulders back and put a little extra hip into her walk, knowing it would make her breasts sway more than normal.

Sure enough, as soon as she breached the circle of light, her chest was exactly what held Roman's attention. His hazel eyes went wide and then hooded. "AC/DC."

"I'm a fan." She looked down and pulled at the hem of her shirt, which drew the fabric forward and revealed a bit more side cleavage. "They're classic."

"How attached are you to that shirt?"

The question brought her head up. She found him closer than before and stopped. "I've had this shirt since I was thirteen."

"Mmm." He circled her, and she didn't bother to try to keep him in sight. Allie already knew what he'd see. The tiny sleep shorts that her ass filled out, the slits in the side teasing even more skin. The carefully ripped sides of the shirt that showed her breasts and part of her side. She normally wore the shirt for sleeping or working out—*with* a bra. It was practically indecent without one.

Which was the point.

Roman stopped in front of her, closer than before. He reached out and ran his hands slowly down her arms, his thumbs caressing the sides of her breasts. "I'll show the required restraint not to rip it off you right this fucking second."

Allie shivered. "If you did, we'd have a problem."

"Noted." His hands moved back up her arms, thumbs again making the movement a tease. "Were you wearing this when you got the note?"

"I might have made a few alterations." *Thanks for the tip, Becka.*

"Mmm." The sound was somewhere between a purr and a growl. Roman released her arms and hooked his fingers into her shorts. A swift yank and they hit the deck. "No panties. Allie, I think you're going to fucking kill me."

She started to pull her shirt off, but he stopped her. "Keep it on. It's just as much a tease as you are."

"If anyone is a tease, it's you."

"Is that so?" Roman undid the ties at the front of his suit and slid it off without taking his eyes from her. "You came earlier, Allie. I suffered."

She smacked his hands away when he reached for her again. "Don't pull that shit with me. You said you'd jerk yourself. If you didn't, that's your problem, not mine." She tried to make herself believe the words. She wasn't some idiot teenager who thought blue balls meant she owed a guy something, but the thought of Roman suffering didn't sit well with her, even if he was the enemy outside of this island.

"If you think my hand can compare to your pussy, you're sadly mistaken." He went to his knees right there in front of her and lifted her shirt to bare her completely from the waist down. "It's been hours, Allie. Fucking *hours* that I've wanted you and haven't been able to do a goddamn thing about it." Roman dragged his mouth from one hip to the other, just below her belly button. He inhaled deeply. "I crave you. What are you doing to me?"

"Me?" She didn't get more than that out before he nudged her legs wider and gave her pussy a long lick. The position didn't leave her open nearly enough, and she tried to spread her legs farther without toppling over.

Roman hooked the backs of her thighs and lifted her to straddle his face. She blinked down at him, but he was too busy taking advantage of the access. He delved his tongue into her, and pleasure made her stop worrying about if he was going to drop her. She clung to his head and gave herself over to what he did to her, trusting him.

He fucked her with his tongue the same way he fucked her with his fingers and cock. Thoroughly. She could barely shift against him in her current position, though, and frustration warred with desire. "Not enough. I need more."

His growl vibrated through her and seemed to center on her clit. He shifted and she let loose a cry as he stood and walked them to one of the lounge chairs arranged to look out over the beach. With the light of the villa, the contrasting darkness felt absolute, but Allie didn't have a chance to think too hard on that before he laid her on the lounge chair and lifted his head. "Not enough."

"That's what I said."

He pushed two fingers into her. One stroke. A second. A third finger joined them. Roman used his other hand to tug her shirt to reveal one breast. He flicked her nipple with his tongue as he plunged his fingers into her again and again. "Is this enough, Allie?"

Yes. No.

She thrashed, shaking her head. "I need *you*."

He nipped the underside of her breast. "You missed my cock. You've been empty and aching for me since you left. That orgasm earlier only made it worse, didn't it?"

"Yes," she sobbed out. It was the truth. Instead of taking the edge off, she'd been acutely aware of what she was missing, rather than what she'd gotten.

"You need me, Allie." He kept up the punishing rhythm with his fingers. "You need what I can give you."

"Yes! I need you." She grabbed his shoulders. "Tell me you have a condom nearby."

She felt his grin against her skin. "I stashed some earlier." He reached under the lounge chair and she heard the familiar crinkle of foil. Roman ripped it open and stopped touching her long enough to roll it on. "Up."

Allie scrambled to obey, already anticipating what came next. He took her place on the lounge chair and guided her to straddle him. "That shirt won't last much longer." He cupped her exposed breast and went still as she positioned his cock at her entrance. "That's it, Allie. Take what you need."

I need you.

She didn't say it again. It felt too big, too vulnerable, to give voice to, when she was going out of her mind with what he was doing to her. She sank onto his length, enjoying teasing them both by taking it slow. Only when he was sheathed completely inside her did she breathe out. "Yes. This."

He pulled her shirt up. "I want to see all of you while you ride me."

There were no shadows to hide in out here on the patio. Anyone who walked up could see them, but that was the point of paradise—there was no one but them. She liked the thought of being interrupted, though—more than she wanted to admit.

Allie took her shirt off, braced her hands on his chest and began to move. A long slide up, and another down while she rolled her hips. It felt so fucking good, she had a hard time keeping up the rhythm. Roman's grip on her hips urged her on, her pleasure cresting all too soon. She dug her nails into his perfect chest. "I'm close."

"I know."

So damn cocky. It would have been unbearable if not for the way he watched her, as if she was something he wanted. Needed. Allie couldn't close her eyes, couldn't look away, couldn't do anything but ride him with one slow stroke after another, pushing them both toward oblivion.

"I love your body." He skimmed his hands over her stomach and up to her breasts. A few breathtaking seconds spent plucking her nipples and then he coasted his hands back down to her ass. "Fucking phenomenal."

"Stop talking." She had decent self-confidence, but that didn't mean his showering her with compliments made her comfortable. Allie knew Roman wanted her—he wouldn't have acted the way he had since meeting her if he didn't. He sure as hell wouldn't have compromised his business plans to give them a reprieve. She might not know him well, but she knew that much. But the way he spoke to her—about her—was as worshipful as if he really thought she was Aphrodite.

But she was only a woman, and not one that he'd like all that much outside of paradise.

Allie might not be sure of a lot of things, but she was sure of *that*.

CHAPTER NINE

ROMAN HELD ALLIE'S BODY, but her mind was a million miles away—just like it'd been since they'd finished having sex. He had no right to push her. He knew that. The agreement that had brought her here in the first place was the same one that kept him from asking anything that might link back to New York.

Except...

"What are you thinking about?"

"Hmm?" She blinked those impossibly blue eyes at him and gave herself a shake. "Sorry. I was mentally wandering."

It was tempting to let it go. Hell, it was the right move to make. But when Roman opened his mouth, that wasn't what came out. "Tell me."

"It's just boring stuff." She shifted off him and climbed to her feet. A small petty part of him was pleased to see her legs shake a little. The sex had been...beyond words. Desperation—that was what he felt for her. He'd hoped she'd respond favorably to the note, but Roman hadn't been sure she'd actually come to him.

He wasn't sure of a lot of things when it came to Allie.

She scooped up her clothes but made no move to pull them on. He liked that. She was so comfortable in her body, and that confidence was just as attractive as her looks were. But all that was surface-level shit. He wanted to know *her*.

Roman stopped short. Knowing her wasn't part of the bargain. It was supposed to be just sex—strictly physical with nothing else involved.

She didn't say no emotion. She said no business. Apples and oranges.

He steadied himself and followed her into the villa. She meandered to the kitchen and pulled a bottled water from the little fridge. Allie watched him as she took a long drink. "What?"

"What?"

She frowned. "Now you're the one mentally wandering. What's going on in that devious brain of yours?"

He grabbed his own water and contemplated it. "I was thinking about the terms of our agreement."

She went still. "And?"

This was the moment he could back off, change course and keep them in a safe spot. But Roman had never met a woman that both turned him on and called him on his shit the same way Allie did. He might never again. Letting her slip through his fingers without at least poking at the potential for more was a stupid move.

Roman didn't make a habit of making stupid moves.

"And I want to know more about you." He watched her closely, noting the tension that crept into her shoulders.

Allie set her water bottle down on the counter. "Why?"

"I haven't connected with a woman the way I've connected with you. Ever. I want to know if it's just lust that will run itself out or if it has the potential to be more."

"Normally..." She shook her head. "There is no normal in this situation. In another world, I'd think that sounded downright nice. But this isn't another world, this is ours—and no matter how great the sex is or how compelling the connection, there remains the fact that you want to buy my business out from underneath me."

"Ah-ah." Roman held up a finger. "No business talk. That was part of the agreement."

She glared. "That was before—" Allie cut herself off and looked at the ceiling. "Damn it, you're right."

"Taking business out of it—"

"Roman, that's crazy."

"You keep throwing around that word. Maybe you're even right." He set his water bottle next to hers and placed his hands on either side of her hips on the counter. "But what if you're not, Allie? Do you run into this kind of thing so often that you're willing to pass it up?"

She frowned harder. "Your argument is compelling. Irritating, but compelling."

He'd given her a lot to think about, but he wasn't planning on giving her recovery time to think *too* much. Roman traced her collarbone. "Any siblings?"

"Only child." Her expression closed off, as clear as if she'd lit a neon sign warning him away.

Family is off-limits. Got it. It was almost enough to confirm that Allie's pushing so hard for the women's shelter had something to do with her past. He set the thought aside—for now. He wanted her to tell him when she was ready. He might have the file on her history, but he decided right then that he wouldn't read it. Better to hear from Allie whatever she wanted to share with him.

What happens when we get back to the mainland?

We'll figure it out.

She pulled her hair off her shoulder to give him a clear path to stroke to her arm and back again. "You have siblings?"

"No. I always wanted one or two, but my parents had other priorities."

"Like what?"

He glanced at her face, but there was only curiosity there. Roman stroked her knuckles. "They're both from old money, and while I was growing up, their only priority was making the family even richer. My old man was a stockbroker, and my mother was a consultant like I am."

"Was?"

He shrugged. "They retired a couple years back. I haven't seen them since, but they bought a boat and have been traveling the world. It's large enough to house a small army, because my parents never do anything halfway. They'll come around again when they get tired of the travel, but I don't expect them to stay. They're nothing if not restless. Always have been." He loved his parents, in a way, but it was a distant sort of feeling that meant talking to them once every few months and the occasional Christmas card if they stayed in one place long enough to receive it. He had friends who'd grown up with loud families filled to the brim with messy love that manifested in jokes and hugs and the occasional heated fight. There was no room for that in the deep stillness of the Bassani household. "Even when I was little, they traveled regularly. They'd be gone for weeks at a time."

"That must have been hard to deal with as a kid." She looped her arms around his neck, bringing them chest to chest. "I don't know anyone with perfect parents—mine included—but at least most of them were *there*. The absent figures must have sucked."

"I thought it was a grand old time when I was in high school. Parties every weekend and girls staying over most days of the week." He tried to give the comment lightly, but it came out bittersweet.

Allie saw it. She smiled and ran her finger along the shell of his ear. "You turned out all right—except for the whole business thing that we aren't talking about."

He laughed. "Except for that—which is my life."

"Seriously? You don't have anything else going on but work?"

He squeezed her hips. "Do you?"

She opened her mouth but seemed to reconsider. "That's a fair point. I could argue that my business is more honorable, but…I'm not in the mood to argue."

Roman liked this side of her, playful and almost coy. He turned them so he could lean against the counter with her in his arms. "What, pray tell, are you in the mood for?"

"I'm so very glad you asked." She kissed his

throat, his shoulder, his pectoral muscle, sliding to her knees in front of him.

The wood floor would be hell on her knees, but she gave him a look from beneath her lashes that stilled the words in his chest. Allie knew exactly what she was doing, and she wasn't about to let him drive the show this time. The sight of her stroking his cock with an exploratory hand had him in danger of swaying. It was only the promise of her wetting her lips that kept him pinned in place.

"Your cock is ridiculous." She gave him another stroke. "There isn't another word. Just *ridiculous*."

He tried to laugh, but the sound came out strangled. "Thanks?"

"You're welcome, but seriously, with you packing this around, it's no wonder you're an arrogant ass." She flicked her tongue along the underside. "You've gone down on me like a dozen times in the last few days and I haven't had you in my mouth even *once*."

"Show me."

She gave him a saucy smile and then his cock was between her lips. Allie sucked him down, down, down, until he bumped the back of her throat. Roman gripped the counter, using every ounce of self-control he had to keep from moving other than to brace his legs a little wider.

She took the move as an invitation and cradled his balls with one hand while she kept sucking him. Just when he thought he couldn't take another second of it, she released him. But Allie wasn't done. She gripped him around the base of his cock with her free hand and licked him like he was her favorite flavor of lollipop. That evil, wonderful tongue of hers damn near made his eyes roll back in his head. "Fuck, Allie."

"We're about to."

Allie barely got the words out before Roman was on her. He paused long enough to pull a condom out of a candy bowl she hadn't noticed before and then he was between her thighs, his cock sliding home. He cradled her head with one of his big hands, saving her from knocking herself silly against the hardwood floor with the strength of his thrusts.

It was…brutal. There was no other word to describe the way he moved over her—in her.

She loved every single second of it.

She was the reason he'd lost control.

Allie clung to him, rising in time with his strokes. "I should give you head more often."

"Every single goddamn day." He kissed her, which was just as well because she didn't have a response to that. *Every day* sounded a whole lot like time after they left West Island. Allie couldn't promise him that. He *knew* she couldn't promise him that.

She kissed him back with everything she had. Their limited time only made the whole thing hotter—or that was what Allie told herself as Roman rolled them. She slammed down onto him without missing a beat, leaning back to brace herself on his big thighs. The man was a monster in the best way possible. The wood floor bit into her knees, but the faint pain only spiked her pleasure higher. She bent down and kissed him without throwing off their rhythm. *Yesyesyesyesyes.*

"After this. Bed."

"Yes."

Roman palmed the back of her head and pressed a hand to the small of her back, effectively caging her. He thrust up, fucking her from below while she was helpless to do anything but take it. Allie took his mouth even as he took her pussy, the pleasure so intense there was no holding out. She came with a cry that he ate down, her legs shaking from the strength of her orgasm. He followed her over the edge with a curse, his rough grip at odds with the sheer pleasure written across his face.

They lay there for several long moments before he shifted her to the side. She gave a small cry of surprise as he climbed to his feet, lifting her into his arms in the process. "What are you doing?"

"We might not be too old to fuck on wood floors, but it's hell on the back." He shifted her and pressed a soft kiss to each of her knees. "And on you."

"Totally worth it."

"Without a doubt." He chuckled. "We'll call the bed a nice change of pace."

But he wasn't going to the bed. He turned left inside the bedroom and walked through the doorway leading into the bathroom. It was similar to the two in her villa, but the coloring was all soft grays and a bright blue that reminded her of the ocean surrounding the island. The tiled walk-in shower was large enough to fit ten people, with two sunflower showerheads and a bench that made her think filthy thoughts despite the exhaustion that broke over her in a wave.

Allie lay her head against his shoulder. "I should get back."

"I don't think so." He set her on the bench. "It's late, and it's dark, and I promise to let you get some sleep tonight if you stay."

She raised her eyebrows. "*Some* sleep?"

Roman turned on the water and shot her a look. "You can't honestly expect me to have you in my bed and keep my hands to myself."

"God forbid." She stood and ducked under the closest showerhead. The water was the perfect temperature, and Allie let herself just *be* for a few seconds. She could hear Roman washing himself, and as tempting as it was to watch, her thoughts kept her feet rooted in place. *He wants to know me*.

The thought shouldn't scare the shit out of her. Roman was gorgeous and successful and... It would never work. Irreconcilable differences about summed them up. Those differences might not matter while they were on West Island, but they would be glaringly obvious when they got back to New York. He was a rich...whatever the hell he was...and she was having to rob Peter to pay Paul and make ends meet. They lived in two different worlds.

They always had.

He'd grown up rich with distant parents. Her heart ached a little for the boy he must have been. So alone. In that, at least, there was a thread of similar experiences. The main difference was that Allie would have given anything for her parents to be gone and leave her alone. Well, her father at least. She shuddered.

"It's okay." His arms slid around her from behind. She tensed, waiting for him to ask what was wrong, but Roman just turned her to face him and held her closer. Comforting her without prying.

Even though she knew better, Allie clung to him. She wasn't weak for wanting to lean on someone for just a few seconds. *It's so hard being*

*strong all the time. I don't know if I can take it.
I'm about to fail, and when I do, I'm going to take
so many women down with me.* Words pressed
against the inside of her lips, all her worries and
fears that she never gave voice to bubbling up inside her. She clamped her mouth shut and buried
her face against his shoulder.

No matter how good the sex, or how wonderful he seemed to be, she couldn't afford to forget what Roman's ultimate goal was—the gym
and shelter. He might have shelved his ambition
temporarily, but that was all it was. Temporary.
Spilling her fears would just give him ammunition later.

What if he could actually help?

He can't. No one can.

Worse, his version of help might be to sell the
damn thing out from underneath her. It wasn't as
easy as that, but once she started missing bills,
it opened a door she couldn't close. If she didn't
figure something out, and fast, she wouldn't have
any choice at all in the matter. *I need a plan...a
better plan than just pushing forward and hoping for the best.*

"It will be okay," he murmured and stroked
a hand down her back. "Whatever it is, it'll be
okay, Allie."

She wished she could believe him.

Allie took a breath, and then another. Self-pity

wasn't her MO. She was the fighter, the one who took people under her wing. She stepped back, and Roman let her go. To hide her embarrassment, she ducked under the spray again. By the time she cleared the water from her eyes, Roman had turned off his showerhead and was drying himself off with an oversize fluffy white towel. He returned with a second one, and she stepped into it after turning off the water.

Roman kissed her forehead. "Come to bed with me, Allie."

Despite the turmoil in her head, there was only one answer. "Yes."

CHAPTER TEN

ROMAN WOKE TO find Allie gone. He sighed and rolled onto his back. It shouldn't have surprised him that she'd bolted, but disappointment was sour on his tongue. He stared at the vaulted ceiling for a few long moments before he forced himself out of bed. Lying around all morning wasn't going to do anything but give him more time to debate what the fuck he was going to do.

Accepting her terms was probably a mistake. But the thought held no strength against the memories from last night. He wouldn't take that choice back, no matter how thoroughly it might bite him in the ass later.

He pulled on a pair of shorts and headed out into the main living space of the villa. It was a sprawling room containing a kitchen and furniture artfully arranged around the wall that opened to the beach. Roman stopped short at the sight of

Allie walking up the steps, sand on her feet and her blond hair windblown.

She grinned. "The sunrise is seriously beautiful today."

She didn't leave. He tried to get his reaction under control and to smile in return. "It *is* paradise."

"That's true." Allie dropped a kiss on his lips as she walked past. "I got coffee started. How do you take yours?"

Roman had never lived with a woman before. Even when he'd dated—occasionally seriously—his schedule prevented this kind of casual morning interaction. It had never felt like a loss until that moment. He followed Allie into the kitchen. "Black."

"I should have known." She'd reclaimed her shirt and shorts, and they looked even better in the daylight than they had the night before. She brought two mugs from the open-faced cupboards and poured coffee into them. After setting his in front of him, she doused hers with enough cream and sugar to make his teeth hurt. She shot him a look from beneath her lashes. "What can I say? I like sweet."

"I see that." Even this early in the morning, he was smart enough not to comment on it. He took a cautious sip. "You stayed."

She stirred her coffee. "I almost left, but it

didn't seem right to sneak out like a thief." Allie made a face. "Plus, Becka was otherwise oc-cupied last night, so I don't expect her up and around until a little later. I do *not* need to walk in on some kind of morning-after shenanigans."

He almost asked, but Roman was... He didn't know how to term his relationship with Becka's sister anymore. They were friends once, albeit not close ones. They might be friends again if Gideon ever forgave him for meddling in their relationship. At this point, he'd be lucky if he was invited to the wedding.

Either way, it was none of his damn business who Becka Baudin went to bed with. He wasn't her brother, and he wasn't her friend. Her sister might have an opinion on that, but Lucy wasn't here and Roman wouldn't win any points by run-ning back to her and telling tales. No, Becka was a grown-ass woman and he was going to stay the hell out of it.

Roman leaned against the counter. "Big plans today?"

"We were going to go snorkeling off the reef on the other side of the island. They have a boat that takes you out and they provide lunch, too." She hesitated. "Do you want to come?"

Yes.

He tempered his reaction almost as fast as it arose. Jumping at her and yanking her into his arms was only going to spook her and make him look like a fool in the process. Instead, he saluted her with his mug. "Only if I'm not intruding."

Allie raised her eyebrows. "As if you'd let that stop you."

He laughed. "Fair point. Yes, I'd like to come snorkeling with you." Saying it felt like he was agreeing to something more serious than a daytime outing, but Roman didn't let himself think about that too hard. He liked Allie. He liked spending time with her. She wasn't going to let him get any ground on talking business while they were down there, and even if he went back to New York, he couldn't make any forward progress without her. All that aside, he *wanted* to be on West Island. With her.

"When's the last time you had a vacation?"

He shrugged. "I visited my parents in Morocco a couple years ago."

Those blue eyes saw too much. She gave a soft smile. "When's the last time you had a real—*relaxing*—vacation?"

"Ah, that's something else altogether." He thought hard and came up blank. "I don't know. Maybe spring break in college, but that's hardly the idea of relaxing you're talking about." He'd had his eye on the prize even back then, so Roman had used the time to network. Nothing brought people together as much as getting drunk and doing stupid shit, and those relationships had panned out nicely in the years since.

But an actual vacation? Just to relax?

He cleared his throat, not quite able to meet her gaze. "Never."

"That's what I thought." Allie set down her mug and slid into his arms as if she'd made the move a thousand times before. "We have four days left on West Island. Why don't we treat it like a real vacation and just enjoy ourselves?"

It sounded a whole hell of a lot like she'd just smacked an expiration date on them. Roman wasn't surprised at that. What *did* surprise him was how her words made him feel—like he wanted to bend her over the counter and fuck her until she admitted that there might actually be something *there*.

Instead, he palmed her ass and gave her a light squeeze. "You'll stay here at night."

"Yes." No argument for once. Her gaze dropped to his lips. "I have to talk to Becka, but judging by how excited she was by my leaving last night, I don't think she'll have a problem with the change of plans. Especially if it leaves the villa open for her to have her own vacation fling."

I'm not a fucking fling.

Once again, he smothered the response. Roman didn't know what he wanted from this yet, other than more time with Allie, but he'd be damned before he did or said something to spook her. There would be plenty of time to hash it out later. Right now, they were just talking about the next four days.

He smoothed her hair back. "Why don't you bring your things here for the duration—it'd save you the multiple trips."

"Trips I'll still have to make to arrange things with Becka for our daily plans." Allie shook her head. "No, this is better with clear boundaries. I'll bring enough stuff for overnight—toothbrush and that kind of thing—but the rest stays."

Stubborn woman.

"You're being difficult."

She grinned. "What I'm being, Roman, is noncompliant. I get the feeling that you don't get told no a lot, but you should get used to it. You might have a magical cock, but that doesn't mean you get a permanent free pass to run my life."

"You think I have a magical cock?" He pulled her closer, lining up their hips so she could feel exactly what she'd just described.

Allie's eyes went wide. "I might have said that." She palmed him through his shorts. "Then again, my memory is a bit faulty. It's been ages since I've had you inside me."

"Woman, it's been a few hours at most." He laughed and scooped her into his arms, liking the little yip sound she made. "But never let it be said that I don't take care of your needs."

"Heaven forbid." She arched up to murmur in his ear. "I'm desperate for you, Roman."

His cock went rock solid and he tightened his hold on her. "In that case, I think your friend can wait another hour or two." He strode for the bedroom.

Allie sat as rigid as she was able to while the boat wobbled its way through the waves away from the island. When she'd invited Roman along to go snorkeling, she hadn't really thought it through. Becka hadn't seemed to mind, so it didn't really sink in until they'd left the island that this was…a date.

No, not a *real* date.

But it was as close as she'd come to a date in *years*.

Not loving what that says about my social life. What social life?

It was different when it was just her and Roman in his villa. She didn't have to think too hard about the implications, because it was clearly just sex. Or maybe the sex just fuzzed her mind and *that* was why spending all that time with him didn't bother her.

Either way, it was different now.

They were out in what passed for public on

the island. The little boat was maxed out with her, Roman, Becka and a trio of giggling women who kept shooting Roman significant looks. All three had wedding rings, but that didn't look like it'd stop them from taking him somewhere to be alone if he so much as crooked a finger.

Allie clenched her fists and stared pointedly at the ocean. Roman wasn't hers. If he wanted to run off with someone else, she didn't have a right to be pissed. She certainly didn't have the right to punch him over it. *Get it together.*

"You look like you're about to shove some-one into the ocean." Roman's murmur was barely loud enough to be heard over the waves they cut through. "What's wrong?"

"Nothing's wrong." She'd answered too quickly. *Might as well have put a sign over my head claiming the opposite.*

"Allie."

She glared at the horizon. If she was smart, she'd fake a smile and play this off. Admitting to feeling something as damning as jealousy would give Roman even more ammunition than he already had. Then again, if she'd wanted to prevent him from having ammunition, she shouldn't have slept with him a second and third time…and she shouldn't be planning on doing it again at the earliest available opportunity. There was no taking back those actions, and she had no intention of stopping until she really had to.

"Allie." He pressed his hand to the small of her back. "You've been checking out on me ever since last night."

"Maybe it's just what I do. You don't actually know me, so you don't know that it's not something I don't do." It sounded just as jumbled as her head felt. She battled the truly ridiculous urge to cry. Allie shook her head. "I'm sorry. I think it all just became real to me and I'm trying to come to terms with the fact that I'm not really protected against you and it's my own damn fault."

Roman moved closer, his body blocking her from the rest of the people on the boat. "You think you need protection from me?"

She couldn't read his tone, but the words didn't sound any happier than she felt. "Not like *that*. I know you'd never hurt me, but…" But once they left West Island, all bets were off. She also knew that. She'd known that going into this thing with him.

So why did it bother her so much now?

I like him.

It was as simple as that. It might have started with just sex, but it wasn't *just* sex. She'd never been all that good at compartmentalizing, and even if she had been, Roman's sheer presence would overwhelm whatever barriers she put up between them. It was easier when she could pretend she loathed everything about him except for his body.

That fallacy hadn't held up against their interaction that morning. He wasn't just an unfeeling suit. He was a man, with a past and a present and a future, and they had at least a few superficial things in common. She understood his loneliness, because she held the twin feeling inside her. He spoke to her as if he cared what she thought, even if most of the time they'd been too busy to talk about much of anything. It didn't matter. That focus was *there* and he'd have her confessing her deepest desires if given half a chance.

She turned to face him, putting her back against the boat railing. His expression wasn't a happy one. He hadn't had a vacation, and she'd invited him out here to continue their feel-good time together...and now she was ruining it. She hated that, hated that she'd been the one to damper his enjoyment of the boat ride. *Of the sight of those women.*

Stop it.

She bit her lip, but there was no holding back the torrent of words. "I hate the way they look at you."

He blinked and then blinked again as comprehension dawned. "You're jealous."

"I wouldn't say *that*." That was exactly what she'd say.

Roman moved closer and skated his hand up her side until his thumb brushed the side of her breast through her swimsuit top. "Do you honestly think I have the slightest interest in anyone else?"

She didn't really know. That was the problem. It was entirely possible that the only reason he'd come onto her the first night was because they were literally the only two people in the restaurant. *Oh, for God's sake,* stop. Allie gave herself a shake. She didn't do this. Crippling self-doubt was exactly that—crippling. She hadn't had time for that nonsense up until this point, and she'd be damned if she would let it prevent her from enjoying her remaining time with Roman.

She took a long, slow breath, and then another. "Okay, yes, I'm jealous. You might not be mine, but you're mine right now, and I don't like them looking at you like you're a piece of meat they'd like to share over dinner."

Roman burst out laughing, the sound taking up residence in her chest…and lower. His thumb dipped beneath her swimsuit, wandering dangerously close to her nipple. "You know damn well that you're the only one who gets to have me for dinner."

She couldn't find the air to laugh. Not when

he pressed his hips into her, letting her know *exactly* how much he wanted her to have him for dinner. Allie ran her hands up his chest. "There isn't anywhere private on this boat."

"If there was, we'd already be there, and I'd be inside you." Roman's thumb found her nipple. "I wouldn't even tell you to be quiet, Allie. I'd fuck you hard enough to make you scream as you came around my cock, so everyone within hearing range would know exactly who it belongs to."

Belongs to.

She didn't know what to say to that, so she went onto her tiptoes and kissed him. Allie looped her arms around his neck and pressed her body against his and tried to tell him without words how hot he made her—how much she appreciated the distraction.

Distantly, she was aware of the boat turning and stopping. The guy driving it cleared his throat. "We'll gear up here and you can explore the reef." He went on, but she was too focused on the heat rising to her cheeks to pay attention.

Roman backed off just enough to fix her top and then slid behind her and wrapped his arms around her waist. His cock pressed against her backside, the hard length preventing her from focusing fully on the instructions. He knew it, damn him. His lips brushed her ear. "Pay attention."

"Stop distracting me." She rolled her hips a little, rubbing her ass against him.

The instructor finally finished up and started handing out snorkels and life vests. Allie slipped out of Roman's grasp and headed for Becka. Her friend gave her a significant look. "I thought you two were going to go at it right there."

Her face flamed, but she tried to laugh it off. "Don't be ridiculous."

"It's not ridiculous if it's true." Becka grinned. "Get it, girl." Her gaze went over Allie's shoulder and her eyebrows inched up. "Would you look at that?"

She turned around in time to see one of the other women saunter up to Roman. Her bikini was tiny enough to border on indecent, and she wore it with utter confidence. Normally, that would have been enough for Allie to want to give her a high five, but with the way the brunette was eye-fucking Roman, the only thing Allie wanted to high-five was her face—with a chair. She sidled up to him, all flirtatious moves and sweet smiles, and placed her hand on his arm, leaning in so her barely covered breasts pressed against his biceps.

He took off his sunglasses and looked down at the spots where she touched him with such coldness that she actually jumped back a step. Roman gave her one last long look that wasn't in the least bit friendly and then turned to take his snorkel gear from their guide. He donned it quickly, dropped his sunglasses on top of his towel and slipped into the water.

All without saying a word.

Becka whistled under her breath. "He gets a nine for takedown, with a plus-two bonus for dramatic exit."

Allie snorted and then tried to cover the sound with a cough. "You're horrible."

"No, what's horrible was that attempt to poach your man." She spoke just loud enough that there was no way the other woman didn't hear her. "Who the hell does that? He was two seconds from dragging you into the ocean to bang you against the side of the boat and *she* thinks she has a chance?" Becka tsked. "Girl's got issues."

Allie smacked her friend lightly even though she agreed with everything Becka had said. All her worries seemed silly in the face of what had just happened. Hell, they were silly even before Roman rebuffed the woman. *A fling in paradise. Don't complicate things for no damn reason.*

Easier said than done.

CHAPTER ELEVEN

ROMAN ENJOYED THE hell out of the day. The weird tension riding Allie disappeared once they got into the water, and they spent several hours exploring the reef and then floating in the waves. By the time the boat dropped them back to the island, she was tucked comfortably under his arm and chatting animatedly with Becka. Roman kept expecting her friend to say…something…about their arrangement, but Becka seemed content to hang out as if this was the most normal thing in the world.

He drove them both back to their villa and left the women there. Though he wanted to take Allie back to his place, he recognized that she needed a little space.

Frankly, he could use a little space himself.

Roman had never been more conflicted in his life. He liked Allie. He wanted to see her succeed. Fuck, he just flat-out wanted her. But she was right this morning. There was a lot more to take into account than what they'd experienced together on West Island.

With that in mind, he strode into his villa and sat down with the papers he'd stashed there the day before. As much as Roman wanted Allie to give him the information voluntarily, the truth of the matter was that she was blocking him. She had her reasons for not wanting to open up, and he respected that, but this wasn't about his growing feelings for her—it was business.

He had to separate the two.

He couldn't afford not to.

She needed his help. She just didn't know it yet. If he let her wait until she was comfortable talking about this stuff with him—*if* that ever happened—the opportunity would pass and she could lose everything.

He needed to know what he'd missed about that damn gym, and he needed to know now. Stomping down on the guilt that tried to dissuade him, Roman sat down and fanned out the papers. He started at the beginning—with Allie and her family.

A story that he'd seen played out before. Alcoholic father. A mother who fled with her child when the abuse transferred to her daughter. A hard life lived, but which didn't stop Allie from graduating from college with honors and very little student debt. She'd worked her ass off to get Transcend up and running with money her mother had left her when the woman passed away three years ago. The shelter was set up under a nonprofit bearing Allie's mother's name.

But a successful nonprofit took a lot of work and shmoozing, and Allie obviously didn't have a taste for it. It didn't bring in enough to cover the costs, so she'd been draining the income generated by the gym—and her own personal savings.

Roman shook his head. It was an easy fix. Pass off the nonprofit to someone else, franchise Transcend and things would even out—and transfer from red back into the black.

So why was she so resistant to the idea?

Once he knew the answer to that, he'd know how to play things. He sighed. *Except it isn't that simple.* This wasn't a prospective client he could manipulate into doing what he wanted without remorse. This was Allie. He didn't want to hurt her, even if it was ultimately for her own good. He wanted her to trust him—to let him help her.

He kept reading. Her abusive father was horrible, but it didn't explain why she was so determined to do this alone. The woman Roman had started to get to know over the last couple days was strong and smart, but not a control freak like he'd expected. That was the only thing that would explain her insistence on not allowing the investor he represented to buy into the company.

Frustrated, Roman flipped through the papers again. Nothing, and he'd essentially breached her trust by doing this search to begin with. *Fuck.* He'd done the basic background on her when he first found the business, but Allie Landers kept her nose clean and, aside from the business's financial records and her school history, he hadn't dug deeper before.

He wished he hadn't now, either.

Roman threw the papers back into the folder and tucked it into a drawer under the kitchen counter. There was no easy answer here. He'd promised that they would leave business in New York, but the only way he could figure out what was stopping her was to *talk* to her... Some fucking businessman he was. He'd painted himself into one hell of a corner with this.

Enjoying their time together was the only option. If he tried to push her, she'd call an end to the whole thing. Allie didn't care about the pending deadline, since she had no interest in selling her business.

Which was a problem, because the whole damn ship was sinking. She'd be underwater inside of six months and then she'd lose everything. If she would just trust him, he could take care of everything. That was the problem, though. Roman knew he wanted what was best for the gym and Allie, but *Allie* didn't know that. It didn't matter how many different ways he tried to tell her, the truth was that he hadn't done anything to earn her trust, and it was doubtful he'd manage that feat sometime in the next four days.

Roman sat there and contemplated it for nearly an hour, no closer to finding a solution by that point than he had been when he'd first started thinking about it.

What the fuck am I going to do?

Come to dinner with me. Dress to the nines.

Allie looked at the masculine scrawl on the note that had been delivered to their villa with the snack Becka had ordered. She felt a stupid grin pulling at the edges of her lips and tried to fight it. A single note from Roman shouldn't be a highlight of her day—especially after the glory that was snorkeling off the coast of the island—but her heartbeat kicked up a notch knowing that he was thinking about her…and planning something for tonight.

"He sent you another note, didn't he?" Becka stepped out of her room, wearing a wrap dress that showed off her legs and lean frame. She'd pinned her blue hair up into a style that could only be described as shabby chic. And she was grinning like the cat who'd eaten the canary. "I don't know if that's adorable beyond measure or cheesy as hell."

"Both." She tried to sound unimpressed, but the stupid smile wouldn't go away. "It's lame."

"It is not lame. He's smitten." Becka eyed her. "You're both smitten."

"I can't be smitten with Roman Bassani. We only have a few days left and then it's back to being enemies again." The thought dimmed her smile like nothing else had been able to. It was strange to think a time would come when she and Roman would be adversaries, but there was no real alternative. He wanted her gym. She would never give it up. End of story—end of them. Nothing that happened while they were on the island would change that.

Becka poked at the snacks that had been delivered and chose a selection of fruit. "You know he has a client who wants to invest in Transcend. Do you know why?"

"For the same reason all the other investors came around when they realized I wasn't making ends meet as well as I would have liked. They think they can jump on the trendy fitness-nutrition combo and franchise it. They don't care about the shelter—and they'd probably cut it out completely if they had control. It's a money pit, after all, and it's not like they're invested in any of those women's futures." Allie shook her head sharply. "No. I can't risk it. Business isn't so bad that we have to give in to the kind of offer Roman and people like him are bringing us. We're doing just fine." *Not really fine at all.* She should have organized a fund-raiser or something for the shelter, but she was so busy running the gym that the thought of adding anything else to her plate was too much to deal with. So she'd put it off.

She was regretting it now.

Too little, too late.

"How do you know?"

She pulled herself back into the present. "What?"

"How do you know what Roman has planned for Transcend?" Becka popped a piece of pineapple into her mouth. "Have you talked about it?"

"No. And we're not going to." At her friend's incredulous look, she glared. "You wanted me to have hot vacation sex, and hot vacation sex includes not talking about work. That's the only condition Roman and I put on this thing, so hell if I'm going to break the rules. It's just going to end in another fight, and this one we might not be able to screw our way out of." She ran her hand over her face. "What am I doing? This whole thing was a mistake."

Becka jumped to her feet. "Oh, no, you don't! I'm sorry I pushed buttons. I thought I was just asking a question." She hurried to Allie and guided her toward her own room. "Go get ready. Then get your ass back in here and have a shot with me for sure mutual courage. Then we'll never speak of this again—at least for the next few days."

"You don't have to be sorry. I'm the one acting batty." She paused just inside her doorway. "I like him."

"I know you do, honey."

She didn't know if that was comforting or worrisome, so she didn't comment on it. She just gently shut the door between them and dug through her suitcase for something that would be qualified as dressing to the nines. She'd packed a couple nice dresses, just in case, and she laid them both out on her mostly unused bed. One was a simple little black dress that was flowy and showed her cleavage to perfection. The other was a two-piece with a stretchy nude pencil skirt and a cropped bustier top that showed a sliver of skin between them. Normally for something resembling a first date, she'd play it safe with the LBD and leave the trendier choice for once she'd figured out if the guy was a douche or not.

But she already knew what Roman was—and what he thought of her.

Allie's grin reappeared. The cropped top and skirt it was.

She took extra time getting ready, styling

her hair in perfect beach waves and keeping her makeup light enough that it wouldn't melt off her face the second she left the villa—or once she and Roman got to whatever he had planned for dessert. She finished off the look with her strappy wedge sandals. With their three-inch heel, she'd be almost as tall as him, and the idea pleased her more than it probably should have. Roman's masculinity wasn't so fragile that he needed her to cut herself down to make him feel better. It was one of the things she liked about him.

I like a lot of things about him.

Stop it.

Becka grinned when Allie walked back into the main area of the villa. "Ooooh, someone has their seductive panties on tonight."

"I'm not wearing any."

Her friend laughed. "Which just serves to support my point. After that little show on the boat earlier, if he doesn't fall on you like a starving man the second he sees you, I'll eat my shoe."

Allie wasn't prepared to take Roman's response to seeing her—whatever it would be—for granted, so she just shook her head and started for the exit. "See you in the morning?"

"As long as by morning you mean after eleven." Becka set her fork and plate in the sink. "Luke is meeting me here after his shift, and I plan to rock him all night long."

"You like this guy?"

Becka shrugged. "I like parts of him. He doesn't have the most stimulating of personalities, but he's got a monster cock and magic hands, so he's perfect for the time and place." Her smile was sunny but didn't quite reach her eyes. "You know me—I don't do that messy emotional bullshit. I like my life how it is. I don't have time for some needy dude expecting me to bend over backward to rearrange it for him."

There was a story there, but in all the years Allie had known Becka, she'd never got to the heart of it. Despite her friend's carefree spirit, Becka had a hard line when it came to anything resembling a relationship. She liked to laugh away the serious stuff whenever they got close to talking about it, and Allie respected the unspoken request to not bring it up.

Then again, Allie hadn't done more than casually date in that time, either, so she wasn't one to talk.

"Shots!" Becka poured vodka into two glasses and passed one over. "To a night of wall-banging sex and living our vacation to the fullest."

They clinked glasses. "Tomorrow, why don't we do something with just us?" Allie suggested.

"Sure…as long as you aren't using me as a shield against Roman." Becka downed her shot without a grimace. "If you want to spend the rest of this trip with him, then you should. I'm more than capable of keeping myself occupied, and it's not like we don't spend more time with each other in New York than we do with anyone else in our lives."

There was no arguing that, but… She took her shot, closing her eyes as the alcohol burned its way down her throat and created a comforting warmth in her stomach. "I don't want to abandon you." She wasn't sure she wanted to be that close with Roman, either. It was already hard to keep the boundaries in her head between them— between the island and New York, between the present and the inevitable future. Getting to know him better would make it worse.

Except…

"I'll think about it."

"Do that." Becka plucked the shot glass from her hand. "Now get out of here. Five bucks says he bangs you right there on the patio."

"You really need to stop making bets about how quickly Roman and I get to banging." But she laughed all the same. She could shelve all her worries about what the future held—at least for a few more days.

Allie would figure out the rest when she got back to New York.

CHAPTER TWELVE

ROMAN HAD EVERYTHING prepared for Allie. A table set up on the patio overlooking the sunset. The food prepped and ready in its various warming plates. Candlelight. The best of intentions.

And then she walked out of the jungle and the blood rushed out of his head and took up residence in his cock. She wore a skintight beige skirt that his hands were itching to slide over, and her little crop top bustier thing offered her breasts up as if begging for his mouth. The sandals had a little heel on them, which only served to highlight the muscles in her legs and…

He rubbed the back of his hand over his mouth. "Fuck, Aphrodite."

Her sweet smile was reward enough, but he wasn't going to be the gentleman he'd planned to be originally. Not with her looking at him with those come-fuck-me eyes and strolling right up to slide her arms around his neck. Her smile widened as she pressed her hips against his. "Hey."

"Hey." He cupped her ass with one hand and her hip with the other, dragging his thumb along the exposed few inches of her upper stomach between the skirt and top. "You look amazing."

"Thanks." She looked him over. "You, too."

It was too hot for pants, but he'd chosen a pair of khaki shorts and a linen button-down that passed as dressed to the nines for island fashion. "Are you hungry?"

"Starving." She hooked her fingers into his belt loops. "But not for food. I've been thinking about you since we were on the boat." She gave a delicate little shiver that had his cock hardening further. "Dinner will hold. I need you now." Allie had his belt undone in the space of a heartbeat and shoved his pants down his legs.

Shock stole his reasoning when he recognized the look on her face. "You're still jealous."

"No, I'm not." She knelt in front of him and wrapped her fingers around his cock. "I was. It wasn't anything you did, and it wasn't anything I have a right to feel, but it was there all the same."

He laced his fingers through her hair. "You're entitled to feeling anything you damn well please."

"Yes, I'm aware."

He watched her lick her lips, his heartbeat

kicking up a notch. She was jealous of the woman on the boat. Roman hadn't bothered to remember her name, but she had been beautiful and confident and someone he might have looked at twice if he wasn't totally and completely wrapped up in Allie. "Do you really think another woman can compare when you're in the room?"

"We were on a boat." She gave him another stroke but seemed content to talk for the time being.

"The point stands."

Allie pinned him with a look. "I'm not interested in competing with another woman for a single damn thing. Life isn't a zero-sum game, and too often we're pitted against each other when it's not beneficial for anyone but the men around us." When he just looked at her, she relented. "*Fine*. I hated seeing her touch you. I wanted to march up and toss her over the railing. I'm not proud of that."

He wished he'd seen the obvious fury in her gaze when it all went down, though it was probably for the best that he hadn't. Roman had no business being pleased with the fact she was jealous, but he was all the same. He slid his fingers deeper into her hair and lightly massaged her scalp. "I'm not interested in anyone but you."

"For the next few days."

For always. He couldn't say it. Even with all

the extenuating circumstances, it was too soon. Roman had never shied away from what he wanted, though—and what he wanted was Allie Landers.

He just had to give her a reason to give him a shot.

Focus.

"Suck me, Aphrodite. Show me how disinclined you are to share."

She arched a perfectly shaped eyebrow. "I find myself very disinclined to share." Allie licked the underside of his cock like a lollipop and then sucked him down.

Roman had to fight to keep his eyes open, to watch her pretty pink lips move over him. She licked and sucked, her gaze never leaving his face. She worked him like she was laying claim to his cock in a way that had lightning sparking at the small of his back and pressure building in his balls. He wasn't going out like that, though. Not without touching her. "Come here." He guided her off him and lifted her onto a chair.

Roman hit his knees and slid his hands beneath her skirt, pushing the soft fabric up. She wore nothing beneath it, and his breath caught in his throat when he found her wet and ready for him. *Not yet.* But a taste couldn't hurt. He hooked her legs on the outside of her chair arms and dipped his head to drag his tongue over her. As long as he lived, he'd never get enough of the taste of Allie on his tongue.

She moaned and arched her back, offering herself further. "Stroke your cock, Roman. For me."

He froze, nearly coming on the spot at her words. *Fuck, woman, I'm keeping you.*

Keeping one hand bracketing her thigh, he made a fist around his cock and stroked hard. He was already close from her sucking him off, but he wasn't about to let himself come before she did. He flicked her clit with his tongue, alternating between circles and those vertical motions that he knew she liked. A frenzy took hold and he devoured her, driven on by her moans and writhing. She was close. So fucking close. His balls drew up, and he fucked her with his tongue, growling against her pussy. Needing more.

Needing *her.*

Allie laced her fingers through his hair, riding his mouth and crying his name as she orgasmed. He gripped his cock harder, roughening his strokes as he followed her over the edge, coming hard enough that he saw stars. He drew back enough to kiss first one of her thighs and then the other, then he pulled her skirt back down over her hips. "Now it's time for dinner."

Allie slouched in her chair, feeling completely boneless. "That's one way to start a meal."

"Mmm. Yes." Roman kissed her stomach and then adjusted her clothing to its correct place. He did up his pants just as efficiently, and she mourned the loss of the sight of him. The man was built magnificently and as good as he looked in clothes, he looked even better out of them.

He set about doling out food onto two plates with an easy, almost professional quickness. When he nudged a crooked fork back into place, she knew it had to be true. "How long were you a waiter?"

"Six years. My parents paid for my college, but they are big believers in working for anything worth having, so the rest was up to me. I handled room and board and books and all the other bullshit expenses that show up when you're in college by working at a local restaurant." He shook his head. "I will never do it again. Lifetime food service workers are either saints or insane, because nothing brings out the asshole in people as much as the little power they think they have when they're out to dinner."

From the comments he'd made, she'd assumed he'd grown up with money, but knowing he'd had to work for at least part of it made her like him better. "Bet you tip really well."

"I can afford to." He shrugged as if that made a damn bit of difference.

Allie examined her food, giving him a brief

break from a subject that obviously made him uncomfortable. *Interesting.* He hadn't minded talking about working the job, but anything resembling evidence that he might be a good guy and he was suddenly closemouthed. She took a sip of wine. "I was a bartender my college years. O'Leary's." She saw from his look that he knew it. "Rich guys are the worst tippers out there— unless they think they have a shot at getting into your pants. Trust me, it's not something that your waitstaff take for granted."

"You don't have to do that."

"Do what?" She set her glass down and gave him her full attention.

Roman studied her. "Convince me that I'm not a total piece of shit. I already know I'm not. I might not be the best guy out there, but I'm a far cry from the worst. I'm solidly average."

Allie snorted before she could stop herself. "Roman, you are many things, but average is not one of them." And she wasn't just talking about the size of his cock. He was obviously driven and smart and clever, and he'd done well for himself.

Even though she knew better, she still asked, "Why are you in this brand of investments? Why not stockbroking or something that—" Allie cut herself off before she could finish that thought aloud. *Why not something that doesn't involve taking from other people?*

From the look he gave her, he knew exactly where her mind had gone. "I know it doesn't seem like it, but I'm not the enemy—not yours and not any of the others whose businesses I help pair up with investors. Most of them thank me in the end."

She had no doubt about that. Roman was hardly a snake oil salesman, but the force of his personality was often in danger of eclipsing all else—like common sense and reason. If he focused the entirety of it on a person, eventually he'd have them convinced that the sky was green and up was down. Even now, *she* was trying to find a way for it to make sense that he was the good guy and not the boogeyman under the bed that she'd assumed for months.

In truth, he was neither the bad guy nor the dream vacation fling—at least not in full. Reality was a lot more complicated.

Allie took a long drink of her wine and poked at the food on her plate. "You understand where I'm coming from with this."

He didn't answer for several beats. "You want to talk about business?"

Did she? The longer they were together, the clearer it became that they'd have to talk eventually—probably before they actually left the island…but she didn't want it to be tonight. She shook her head. "No. I'm sorry I brought it up."

Another of those searching looks. "We can talk, Allie. We're both adults, and as much as I enjoy the hell out of fucking you, I want to get to know you better."

That sounded like... She didn't know what that sounded like. It didn't fit in with her preconceptions of their boundaries. It didn't fit with *anything*. Allie swallowed against the panic welling inside her. It was just a conversation. She wasn't agreeing to anything just because she was talking with him. She'd *been* talking with him this entire trip. It just felt different this time.

Meaningful.

She took a breath, and then another. "Do you have...hobbies?"

Roman smiled gently, as if he knew what the question had cost her. "I work a shit ton, so I don't have much in the way of time. But I box a couple times a week at my gym—nothing crazy or competitive. Just sparring."

She could see it. He certainly had the upper body of a boxer, though his legs were just as solid as the rest of him. "Boxing and yoga. That's quite the combination." He was experienced with yoga. She'd been doing it for years, and she still had trouble with some of the poses he'd pulled off the other morning.

"They both help with my stress level, albeit in different ways."

"I bet they do." She cocked her head to the side. "Doesn't leave much time for social stuff." Like recognized like—between running the gym and teaching classes, she had nothing in the way of free time.

"How did you get into the gym business?" He held up his hand before she could speak. "I'm not talking about your business right now—I want to know why you chose that route."

She started to consider how she wanted to answer that, but exhaustion rolled over her. Allie was so damn tired of having to watch what she said around him. If she trusted Roman enough to give him full control of her body, she should trust him enough to have a conversation without worrying that he'd twist it around to use it against her.

Maybe it was time for a tiny leap of faith.

Allie took a bite and chewed slowly, finally swallowing the food, though she couldn't have begun to guess what it was she'd eaten. Her entire focus was on Roman and their conversation. He had no way of knowing that the seemingly innocent question would open a whole Pandora's box of history for her. She finally set her fork aside. "When I was growing up, I didn't have the healthiest of childhoods. It could have been a lot worse than it was, but the only high points during those years were when my mom would let me tag along to the gym. When she was there, she was…" She had to search for the word. "Free. In control in a way that she never was while married to my dad. When that relationship ended for good, it was a new city, a new gym, a new sense of purpose. It was in that place that I saw her find herself again, make friends, start the long road to what healthy looked like."

She tried a nonchalant shrug, but every muscle in her body was tense. "I initially started going so we would have something in common, but I really liked it. I never got super into the nutrition aspect of it, but I eat healthy enough." She motioned at her body. "I like food. I like working out. I like giving women like my mom a safe place. It all came together in Transcend."

Roman was so still, he might not have breathed the entire time she spoke. "I'm sorry your father was such a piece of shit."

"Me, too." Once upon a time, she'd wondered if her being born was the thing that ruined her parents' relationship, but Allie had seen too much—heard too many stories out of the same playbook—for that guilt to hold any water. Her father would have been the same if it was a different woman, whether there was a child or not, regardless of the external stressors he liked to blame for his flying off the handle.

She looked at Roman and tried to picture him drinking so much he actually hurt a woman—

anyone, really—and couldn't wrap her mind around it. Maybe she was being naive, because he had a ruthless streak a mile wide, but nothing about him rang that warning bell. *Why am I even thinking about this?*

Because you can't afford not to.

Except this ends when we go back to New York, so it won't matter what he's like when he's not on vacation because you won't be around to see it.

The thought had her sagging in her seat. She poked at her food again. Wanting more with Roman was out of the question. The whole condition of their being together was *not* to talk about the most important thing in their respective lives—her gym and his work. It wasn't sustainable.

But part of her wanted it to be.

CHAPTER THIRTEEN

ROMAN SAW THE exact moment Allie started to shut him out. He'd been pushing it with that question and he'd known it, but there was too much he didn't know about her. He *should* be prodding her with questions to help spin things to his advantage, but the only reason Roman had asked was because he genuinely wanted to know.

He cleared his throat. "I envy you, in a way."

"Why's that?" The distance in her blue eyes retreated, leaving her present and accounted for.

In for a penny, in for a pound. She'd bared part of herself with that little window into her past—he couldn't do anything less than the same. "I mentioned before that my parents weren't around much when I was a kid." He snorted. "I might have understated it. They were gone more often than they were there. There was nothing traumatic about my upbringing, other than a bit of benign neglect, but when I was younger, I would have given my left arm to have designated time with either of them like you had with your mom."

Allie leaned forward, now fully engaged. "Why didn't they have more kids, if only to give you someone who wouldn't leave?"

"My mother didn't like being pregnant all that much, and she wasn't a fan of what came after, either." He made a face. "Hearing that at the tender age of five was eye-opening, to say the least."

"Oh, Roman."

"No, none of that." He casually slashed his hand through the air. "I don't need pity any more than you do. All my needs were met and my parents loved me in their own way. They just loved each other and travel a bit more. I had a whole staff of people who ensured I didn't turn out a monster, though I wager my nanny, Elaine, would feel differently if she'd lived to see me as a business acquisitions consultant." At her raised eyebrows, he continued, "She found money to be a necessary evil but always told me that she hoped I'd pick a good honest job that didn't revolve around it."

He hadn't thought about that conversation in over a decade. Elaine had passed when he was in his first year of college, and by that time he was firmly in his rebellious stage. Too much drinking, too many girls, too many attempts to do something crazy enough to force his parents to acknowledge him. Elaine's death had snapped him out of it like being thrown into a freezing ocean. He'd taken a good hard look at his life and realized that the only person he was hurting was himself. His parents would never change who they were, and trying to push them to be different was a lesson in futility.

Roman shook his head. "This got heavy. Sorry."

She tucked a lock of hair behind her ear. "I appreciate your sharing. It's kind of strange that we don't know much about each other, but…" Allie motioned between them.

"We fuck like we were made for each other." He wished he could recall the coarse words the second they were out of his mouth. He and Allie had bypassed mere fucking days ago. This was something on another level and cheapening it was a shitty thing to do.

She smiled. "Exactly that."

It stung that she agreed with him so quickly, but had he really expected anything else? In an effort to distract them both, he said, "So how did you meet Becka?"

As she launched into a tale of two broke college students desperate enough to take second jobs at the scary campus gym, he sat back and indulged in watching the animated way she spoke. Allie really was beautiful. He'd known that, of course—he had two eyes in his head, after all—but she was beautiful right down to the core. A genuinely good person.

Let me help you.

He couldn't say it. Even talking about the gym in more abstract forms had caused her to shut him out. Trying to talk more explicitly was a recipe for disaster. He had to play the game within the terms they'd set out. It was the only way.

"You're not even listening." She didn't say it like she was mad—just stating a fact.

"I am." Roman managed a smile. "That boss you had at the campus gym sounds like a real piece of work—though he should have been reported for forcing you to be in those conditions."

She raised her eyebrows. "Okay, that's a neat trick. You were a million miles away, but you still retained everything I said. That's nuts."

"Necessary evil." Though he'd never once been called on it before now. "I learned early in my career that it's best to have several options for plans by the end of a meeting with a new client—that means listening to what they're saying while still thinking strategically to create a game plan. They fill out preliminary information, of course, but until I meet them face-to-face, I rarely know exactly what they're looking for." He shrugged. "Some things sound better on paper than they are in reality."

Allie bit her bottom lip, and he could see the conflict clear on her face. "Okay, I'll bite—tell me about your job. Broad strokes, please."

Easy enough, though he couldn't help feeling it was a test. "I am a glorified numbers monkey. I research various businesses that look like good investments and then line up investors that will fit well with them. The ultimate outcome varies. Sometimes they take it to the ground level and build it up again. Sometimes they expand. Sometimes they franchise. Usually it's successful for both business and investor and I get a nice fat bonus."

"Depends on your definition of *successful*, doesn't it?"

He knew where she was going with this, and as much as he didn't want to fight, maybe it was better to get it out there now and expose the elephant in the room. "I won't pretend that every business owner is thrilled with the process, but most of the time the alternative is rock bottom and losing everything they worked their ass off to accomplish. Sometimes compromise is necessary."

She looked directly at him with those big blue eyes. "And do you ever compromise, Roman?"

Allie should have…well, she should have done a lot of things. She regretted the question as soon as she put it to voice—like she regretted much of what she'd said around Roman since they'd met. She pushed to her feet. "Never mind. We just got through saying we shouldn't talk about this—should keep it light—and we keep doing the exact opposite of that."

There was one thing they were good at—better than good at.

She slid her thumbs into the band of her skirt and pushed it down in a smooth move. The top took a little more effort, but she managed to unhook it and drop it without looking like a total fool. Roman hadn't moved once, but his knuckles were white where he held on to the table. He managed to tear his gaze from her breasts to her face. "What are you doing?"

"We're going to ruin this by talking too much. I don't want to ruin it."

Still, he didn't move. "It's okay for us to disagree on things. It's unrealistic to think that we'd match up on every subject the way we match up physically."

She knew that. Of course she knew that. Only a child or an idiot thought there was such a thing as a perfect relationship. Everyone had problems, though most of the time they weren't as catastrophic as her parents' had been.

But this wasn't a relationship. She had to keep reminding herself of that, and *that* was as much a problem as anything.

She shook her head. "That's the thing—this is fantasy. There is no room for disagreements in fantasy. I want you. You want me. Let's just leave it at that."

"Allie—"

She turned and strode into the darkness. He'd follow. He'd be unable to help himself. And then they'd get their hands on each other and all her conflicting feelings would disappear for a while. *That* was what she wanted. She already had a complicated life. She didn't have room for *more* complications—even if they arrived in a package that made her body ache and her heart beat too hard.

Sex was easier. Sex was safe.

Even if it didn't feel particularly safe as she hit the sand and kept going. The wildness of the island was closer to the surface here, with the villa lights seeming at a distance and the stars a blanket overhead. The soft shushing sound of the water sliding over the sand let her draw her first full breath since she and Roman had started talking about things better left unsaid.

She tilted her head back and inhaled deeply, taking the salty air into her lungs and letting it chase away her worries. She was still on vacation, no matter how stubbornly real life kept trying to intrude. Relaxation was the name of the game and

Allie would be damned if she was drawn back into all the crap before she was good and ready.

Footsteps padded behind her, and she didn't turn to watch Roman approach. She wouldn't be able to see more than the outline of him, and it was better to soak up what little peace she could as she waited to see if he'd let the conversation go.

He stopped next to her, close enough that his shoulder brushed against hers. "You can't run from this forever."

"I'm not running from anything." *Liar.* "I'm holding to the arrangement we made. Everything can wait until we leave West Island." What happened then... No, she wasn't going to talk about it. She wasn't even going to *think* about it.

"Allie..." His exhale was lost in the sound of the small waves hitting their feet. "This is what you really want? For me to fuck you until neither of us is capable of words and we just ignore everything unspoken between us?"

This was the moment of truth. If she said she'd changed her mind about their bargain, she had a feeling Roman wouldn't judge her for it. He seemed to want to talk—actually talk. Maybe he was starting to feel the same thing she was— that this thing between them wasn't just about mutual orgasms.

That maybe it could be more.

All she had to do was tell him that she was willing to talk.

But when she opened her mouth, it was cowardice that won. "We can talk when we're in New York."

He turned to face her, his expression lost in the darkness. "Promise me that we will."

"What?"

"Promise me that you won't run when we get back. You'll have dinner with me and we'll talk."

It'll never happen. It sounded good in theory right now, beneath the stars and with their bodies gravitating toward one another, but once they got back to the city and were grounded in their real lives, it wouldn't hold up. He'd get busy. She'd have to cancel a few times. They'd both lose interest and move on with their lives.

The thought made her chest ache, but she set it aside just like everything else she'd set aside since she came here. "I promise."

Roman shifted closer, sliding his hands over her hips and up her back, fitting her body against his. He'd stripped before following her out here, and all his skin against all of hers sent a delicious thrill through her. He kept calling her beautiful, but he was a work of art. "Adonis."

"Aphrodite." He lifted her easily so she could wrap her legs around his waist. "Let's go swimming."

She didn't protest as he walked them into the ocean. Roman didn't go far, stopping as the water lapped the bottom of her breasts. It felt absolutely wicked to be out here in the dark with him. Even if it'd been broad daylight, no one would have seen them, but the thrill of the risk still heightened every sensation.

The water teasing her breasts. The slick slide of his skin against hers. The feel of his breath ghosting across her lips.

She arched against him, trying to take his mouth, but Roman dodged her kiss. "Do you know the legend of Aphrodite?"

She blinked. "Yes, of course. She came from the sea." The words were barely past her lips when Roman launched her away from him. She was airborne for a single breathless second and then she hit the water and went under.

Allie surfaced with a curse that turned into a laugh. "You're crazy."

"Come on. You can't skinny-dip in the Caribbean without horsing around a bit." He splashed her and then disappeared beneath the surface.

Allie skittered back, searching the inky water for a sign of him, but the only warning she got was a hand around her ankle and then he pulled her under. They twisted beneath the surface and tangled together. She used his shoulders to shove him farther down and push herself up for a breath.

And then his arms were around her waist and he was hauling them closer to shore. His cock pressed against the small of her back and her breath hitched in her throat. "Playtime's over."

She laughed at the cheesy line, but the sound came out strained. "You just wanted to get me all wet."

"Mmm." He cupped her breasts and rolled her nipples between his thumbs and forefingers. "Come on. As much as I need you right here, right now, the condoms are back in the villa."

She almost threw caution to the wind and said it didn't matter. Allie clamped her mouth shut to keep the words inside and nodded sharply. Unprotected sex with Roman, no matter how much she wanted him in that moment, was the worst possible idea. "Yes. Villa. Now."

Before she did something they'd both regret.

CHAPTER FOURTEEN

ROMAN CARRIED ALLIE across the sand. He ignored the tension bleeding into her body the farther they got from the waves. *Too much time to think.* They were being so damn careful not to edge too close to subjects that would put them at odds with each other, but he craved that part of her as much as he wanted the rest. Allie wasn't just the beautiful siren who looked so at home in the sun and sand, with the turquoise water creating the perfect backdrop.

She was a strong woman who hadn't let circumstances beyond her control beat her. She'd fought tooth and nail to accomplish so much in such a short time, and it was a fucking tragedy that it hadn't gone according to plan. He didn't want her to lose Transcend any more than she wanted to lose it, if only because he now recognized the pain it would cause.

Roman would go to extraordinary lengths to save Allie from whatever pain he could.

He padded up the porch steps and headed straight for the bedroom. She wouldn't thank him for ruining their good mood with serious talking, and she might go so far as to leave if he tried to broach the forbidden topic. There wasn't a damn thing Roman could do to change that, and he wasn't used to being so effectively painted into a corner.

He couldn't use words to reassure Allie.

But he could use his body.

"Roman?" The hesitance in her tone killed him.

He set her on her feet but didn't release her. Naked and wet from the ocean, she really did look like a siren who'd been sent to tempt him. Allie blinked those big blue eyes. "Are we okay?"

"Yeah." *Not as okay as I want us to be.* He *liked* Allie. He admired her strength. He wanted to bolster it, to be the immovable object she could lean on when she needed it. If there was one thing he was sure about when it came to the woman in his arms, it was that she didn't allow herself to rest, to pass the burden on to another.

He wanted to bear all her burdens, at least for a little while.

Roman framed her face with his hands and stroked his thumbs over her cheekbones. "I want it to be just us while we're here. No past, no worrying about the future. Just you, Allie, and me, Roman. Two people enjoying their time together."

"That sounds good." She bit her bottom lip. "But I don't know if it's possible to just put all that aside and pretend it's not there."

"Aphrodite." He kissed the spot on her lip where there was still an indent from her teeth. "Nothing exists but us. The goddess of love and her Adonis."

She laughed a little. "You know that myth didn't end happily, right?"

"It's Greek mythology. There are no happy endings." He shifted to kiss her stubborn chin. "Fuck them. This is our story."

Her hesitation was so brief, it might not have existed. "Yes. Tonight. The next three days. You and me. I'm in."

As much as Roman didn't want any kind of limit, he knew when not to push his luck. Allie had given him more than he'd hoped, and he'd have to be happy with it. "I'm taking you to bed now."

"Finally." She gave a dramatic sigh. "I thought we'd never get to the good part."

"All of it is the good part." He walked her back to the bed and laid her down, leaning over her. "Tell me what you want. Your wish is my command tonight."

"Just tonight?" There it was again, the slightest hint of vulnerability.

Not just tonight. Always. Promises he had no business making rose, pressing against the inside of his lips like live things. He'd known he wanted Allie, but the realization that he had only three days left with her pulsed up inside him, desperation building with each heartbeat. He looked down at her, her open expression of need cleaving into his chest as if she'd actually struck him. *I don't want to lose you.* He swallowed hard. "We'll start with tonight and see how it goes."

Her grin brought out an answering one from him. "Kiss me, Adonis." She arched up, pressing all of her body against all of his. "Touch me. Hold me. Fuck me."

There was no room in this night for fucking. They'd passed that point days ago, though he couldn't pinpoint the exact moment when Allie went from a gorgeous woman who drove him out of his mind to a woman whose inside was just as compelling as how she felt when she rode his cock. It wasn't just sex between them, no matter what lies she told herself.

Maybe it never had been that uncomplicated.

Roman joined her on the bed and kissed the long line of her neck. "Here." He shifted to the side so he had full access to her body, and moved to the curve of her shoulder. "Perhaps here."

She shivered. "I could think of a few places I'd like."

"I bet you could." He urged her onto her side so he could fit himself against her back. The position gave him free reign, and he wasted no time cupping her full breasts, weighing them in his hands. "Open your eyes."

She obeyed and froze when she met his gaze in the reflection of the windows across from the bed. The deep darkness outside and the single lamp he'd left on inside created a mirror of the glass.

Roman pressed an openmouthed kiss to the back of her neck and retreated just enough for his breath to ghost over the damp skin. She shivered and arched her back against him, pressing her breasts more firmly into his hands. "That feels good."

"I'm just getting started." He lightly pinched her nipples, rolling the tight buds between his fingers. "I love how rosy your skin gets when you like what I'm doing to you."

She lifted her head and frowned. "The reflection isn't that damn good."

"No. It's not." He skated a hand down her stomach and hooked her thigh, lifting her leg up and setting her foot behind his legs. It left her open for him and he delighted in her shiver. "Cold?"

Allie reached back to run her fingers through his hair. "I'm burning up. Touch me, Adonis."

He loved it when she called him that. It was something they alone shared. Something special and meaningful. Roman dragged a single fingertip over the inside of her thigh, teasing her. "Where do you want me to touch you?"

"You know where."

"Mmm. I might." He palmed her pussy, and cursed when he found her warm and wet and wanting. "This is where you want me." He traced her opening. "Where you're aching with need."

"Yes." She shifted her hips to guide him, but he nipped her shoulder. Allie hissed out a breath. "Bossy."

"Always." He spread her wetness up and over her clit and circled the little bud of nerves with the pad of his finger. "You love it."

"Maybe."

"Definitely." Roman pushed two fingers into her, stroking her leisurely while he watched her face. Her sinful lips parted and her blue eyes went hazy. "My Aphrodite." He released her long enough to reach over and snag a condom.

"Let me." Allie turned in his arms and plucked it out of his hand. She ripped it open and then gripped his cock. A stroke. Two. The desire in her eyes a match to the furnace inside him. "You shouldn't be this perfect, you know? It's got to be a mathematical improbability."

He barked out a laugh. "Not perfect. Never

that." He had more than his share of faults. He always had. Too selfish. Too driven, often at the expense of his relationships. Too stubborn by half.

"Well, obviously." She rolled the condom over him, taking her time. "I was talking about your cock, Adonis."

That surprised another laugh out of him despite the fact she started stroking him again. "Quite the backhanded compliment."

"Only if you want to look at it that way." She nudged his shoulder, pushing him onto his back. Allie climbed on top of him and ran her hands up his chest. "Seriously, though. You don't have a single physical imperfection. I've never had a man take my breath away just by looking at him, and you do."

He looked at her, this woman that he'd never planned on. She was trying so fucking hard to keep as many barriers up between them as she could. Easier to focus on the physical than to admit that he might not be as evil as she'd assumed. To admit that she liked him for more than his ability to make her come hard enough to see stars.

Allie positioned his cock at her entrance and sank onto him in a slow movement. Her eyes fluttered closed and her pink lips parted. "Oh, God." She rolled her hips a little, adjusting. "I always think I can anticipate how good it will feel, and I'm always wrong."

"Because it's me."

Her eyes flew open and she frowned down at him. "What?"

"You lose your fucking mind every time I touch you because it's me. Just like I can't keep my god-damn hands to myself when I'm in the same room as you. We make each other crazy, and yeah, some of that has to do with how smoking hot you are. But it's more and you know it." He reached be-tween them to circle her clit with his thumb. "I'm not a glorified dildo or a blow-up doll. I'm *me*."

Allie stared down at Roman. All she wanted was to lose herself in the perfection of the moment, of how good it felt to have him inside her, his big body between her thighs. She didn't want to turn this into something it wasn't supposed to be. *Too little, too late.*

"I know it's you." As if she could detach the man from his body. She couldn't. She'd tried. Ro-man's personality was just as overwhelming as his good looks. "Damn it, I see you."

Driven by the pounding pleasure in her blood, she shifted, swirling her hips a little in a move that made them both gasp. "I see you," Allie re-peated. "You're not a bad man, no matter how much you pretend to be." He might not be a *good* man, but that wasn't something she could deter-mine inside of a week.

Liar.

She leaned down to kiss him, answering the temptation of his mouth as much as she wanted to silence the little voice inside her. *You won't be able to take this back. It's already complicated and it's only going to get more so.* She didn't care. She'd worry about complications when she came to them. All that mattered in that moment was removing the flicker of hurt she'd seen in Roman's hazel eyes.

She tasted the ocean on his lips, felt the warmth of the sun in his skin. Roman was like this island personified, beautiful and more than a little bit wild beneath the carefully cultured exterior.

"It stopped being just sex with you. You know it. I know it. We're still not talking about it."

He hesitated but finally nodded. "I can play the patient hunter, Aphrodite. We won't talk about it tonight. Maybe not for the next three days. But we *will* talk about it."

That was what she was afraid of. "Guess you really *are* Adonis," she murmured against his lips.

"Only when it comes to my Aphrodite."

She didn't want to talk anymore. Every time he'd spoken tonight, he'd chipped away at the fragile balance she'd worked to keep in place. Boundaries were there for a reason and, damn it, Roman seemed determined to trample all over them. He'd stopped playing by the rules, but he hadn't pushed so hard that she could call him on it.

Do I even want to call him on it? What's the harm in enjoying this?

It won't last.

What if it does?

She kissed Roman again, pressing her body into his. She rode him slowly, not worried about the destination. They'd get there eventually. They did every time. No, right now what Allie wanted was to be fully present in the moment. Right there. With him. The rest of the world could wait.

He dug a hand into her hair and grabbed her ass with the other, guiding the long slide of her strokes. Sweat slicked their skin, and the drag of her nipples across his chest made her moan. *So good. Everything* about them was *so good.* Nothing else mattered but how his tongue moved expertly against hers, the feeling of him inside her, big and full and almost too much, and where he would touch her next. "I need more."

He rolled them, and the second her back hit the soft mattress, Roman began to move. He rolled his body like the waves they'd just been playing in. Smooth and steady and hitting all the right places. He ground his pelvic bone against her clit, the friction drawing a moan from her lips. His big body kept her pinned even as he wrapped himself around her. All she could feel was Roman.

All she knew was Roman. The feel of his strong hands gripping her hips, the pounding of his cock between her thighs, the little curses he uttered with each exhale.

Glorious. So incredibly glorious.

"Yes. *There.* Don't stop."

"Come for me, Aphrodite," he growled against her neck. "Come for your man."

She was too lost to the pleasure of what he was doing to her to think too hard on his words. Or that was what she told herself as she buried her face in the curve of his neck and orgasmed hard enough to shake the earth on its axis. Roman pounded into her, wild with a need she felt to her very soul.

This isn't going away. I don't know if it's real or not...but I want it to be.

Roman tucked her against him and held her tightly, as if he expected her to leap out of bed and flee into the night. Considering how hard her heart pounded in a way that had nothing to do with the outstanding sex, she wasn't sure his fears were unfounded. "I don't know how to do this."

"Do what?"

She kept her face pressed against his chest. It was easier to be honest when she wasn't looking directly into those hazel eyes. "This. You. Us." *Us.* One little word, but it somehow changed everything. The realization that this wasn't simple vacation sex had been growing inside her every time Roman touched her. Every time she came with his name on her lips.

He smoothed a strand of her hair back from her face, tilting her head up so she could see him. "Why do you have to do anything at all?" There was something in his expression, something tight and guarded despite his warm smile.

"What's wrong?"

He hesitated and sighed. "Look, Allie, I like you. A lot. But I can tell that this whole thing freaks you out, so I'm trying to not put any pressure on you while we're here."

While we're here.

They wouldn't be on West Island forever. Hell, they wouldn't be here this time next week. This thing they had was temporary. She knew it and he knew it. Allie took a careful breath as the knowledge settled in her chest like a stone. They had an expiration date. There would be a time in the very near future when she'd no longer have the right to spend her nights tangled up with Roman.

I have to shore up enough memories during these last few days to last me a lifetime.

The thought made her want to cry, but she shoved the feeling down deep. There would be plenty of time for tears later. Right now, the only thing that mattered was gorging herself on everything Roman. On the little touches. On his kisses.

On the feeling that rose inside her as she came apart around him.

"Aphrodite?"

She tangled her fingers in his hair and pulled him close for a desperate kiss. She put all her frustration and fear into the slide of her tongue against his. Three days. She had so much living to pack into three tiny twenty-four-hour periods.

Roman pulled her closer yet, his big hands cupping her ass and grinding her against him. He broke the kiss to nip at her jaw. "This is what you need, isn't it? Not to think anymore."

"Yes." He always seemed to know what she needed, even when she couldn't put it into words. "I just want to feel you. To be here and present and not worried about what happens when we get back to New York."

"Consider it done." He captured one of her nipples in his mouth, sucking hard. "Trust me, Aphrodite. I'll take care of you."

For the next three days, she finished silently, even as he rolled her onto her back and began kissing his way down her body. She couldn't bear to think about what happened after.

So she didn't.

CHAPTER FIFTEEN

ROMAN SMOOTHED ALLIE'S hair back from her face. "You'll have to get moving if you're going to make your flight."

She swatted at his hand without opening her eyes. "Screw it. I'm not going back to New York. I'll just stay here until they kick me out."

He felt the same way, though it wasn't the island that had Roman wishing he could make this moment last forever. He wasn't ready to let this thing with her go. It was a truth he'd been working toward for some time, but this morning, knowing that they were going to board their respective flights back to New York and go back to their normal lives… The stakes were suddenly sky-high. "Come out with me tonight."

"What?" She finally opened a single eye. "What are you talking about?"

"Tonight. After we're both settled. I want to take you on a date." He didn't exactly form it as a question, but Roman knew all too well how fragile the limb he stood on was. They'd spoken about changing the rules, but he'd just thrown every single one of them out. Roman stroked his hand down her arm and laced his fingers with hers. "I'm not ready for this to be over."

"Roman, we talked about this. Our lives don't match up outside of this island. Our worlds are too different—our world*views* are too different. We wouldn't last the week before something happened that ruined us for good." She shifted to look down at their joined hands. "And that's not even getting into the whole 'your investor's trying to buy my gym out from underneath me' thing."

She was determined to see the worst in that situation, and he hadn't had the chance to convince her otherwise because every time it came up, suddenly they were having sex. Roman knew damn well that Allie was trying to keep them both distracted, and he couldn't exactly be pissed at the side effect, but he wanted to *talk* to the infuriating woman. "Have dinner with me. We'll talk about all the shit we've been avoiding up until now. If at that point you're sure you don't want me to facilitate someone investing in the gym, then I won't."

"Just like that?"

"Just like that." It wouldn't be just like anything. His client was interested in the gym and she had a clear vision over what she wanted for its future—a vision Roman shared. It wouldn't be easy to find a replacement, but he'd make it work. *If* Allie actually talked to him. "What do you say?"

Still, she hesitated. He could practically see her weighing her desire not to go to that dinner against the chance to get him to back off once and for all. Finally, Allie nodded. "I can't do tonight, but tomorrow I'm free."

"Tomorrow it is." He pressed his lips to her forehead. "As much as I want to seal this with a kiss, if I start kissing you, we won't stop until lunch and you have a plane to catch." He bit back the impulse to tell her to stay—that they really could just live on the island indefinitely and leave their lives behind. That peace wouldn't last. No matter how effectively they'd checked out of reality for the week, given enough time, real life would come creeping into their time here. Hell, it already had. Allie had done her best to avoid it, but Roman was a realist—they needed to get their shit out in the open so they could deal with it.

They had no chance of a future without that.

Before he could reconsider kissing Allie, she was out of the bed and pulling her clothes on. "I'd better go. If left to her own devices, Becka will pack my stuff and her version of packing is to shove everything in and wrestle with the bags until the zipper is in danger of breaking. Better for both me and my luggage if I do it myself."

"Give me your number."

Again, the slightest of hesitations. She grabbed a piece of stationery from the nightstand and scrawled her number on it. "See you tomorrow."

Tomorrow. In New York.

No matter how much he wanted to pretend otherwise, it was a big fucking deal to bring their budding relationship home. Roman managed a smile. "Have a safe flight."

"You, too." And then she was gone.

He listened to her footsteps leading out of the villa, and only after they'd faded did he climb out of bed and throw on a pair of shorts. His flight was in a couple hours—the early one off the island— so he wouldn't have a chance to see Allie again beforehand.

It took fifteen minutes to pack everything he'd brought and comb every room twice to ensure he didn't miss anything. He took extra time to shred up the information he'd gotten about Allie. He didn't need it. She'd given him everything when she spoke about why she'd started the gym. He knew what pressure points to push to incite the reaction he wanted…but he couldn't do it.

She wasn't just a stubborn business owner who needed a little pressure to do things his way. This was *Allie*. For her, he'd bypass the manipulations and shady dealings for plain old honesty.

Roman grabbed his bags and made his way to the lodge. It was time to get this show on the road, and he had a shit ton of work to do on the trip. All the pieces had to be in place before he saw Allie again.

The stakes were too high for it to be any other way.

Allie couldn't wrap her mind around being back in New York. It was more than the weather, more than the sheer amount of people. It was almost like her life didn't quite fit the same way it used to, as if it was a sweater with a tag she'd never noticed before but that itched every time she moved. To distract herself, she taught an early-morning spin class and spent the rest of the day holed up in her office going over bills and the budget for next month.

It was a shitty distraction. Nothing lined up. They'd taken their usual summer months hit in attendance to the classes, which meant less income. She was already in the red, but both the gym and the shelter were rapidly reaching the point of no return. Allie would have to start laying off her girls soon—like next week—and the thought made her sick to her stomach. The only other option was to turn away some of the women

in the shelter, which wasn't an option at all. It was
like having to choose between two of her children and she didn't even know where to begin.

She set it aside to work on later. She couldn't
call Becka, because Becka would quit on the
spot. She wouldn't worry too much about finding another job—Becka was the type of woman
to jump out of a plane and figure out how a para-
chute worked on the way down. It was part of
her charm, but Allie couldn't ask her to make
that decision.

No, who she really wanted to call was Roman.
They'd spoken briefly last night—mostly to arrange a time and place for their date today—but
it was nowhere near enough after having him
within arm's reach for a full week. She wanted
to be wrapped up in him and have him tell her
that it'd all be okay and that they'd figure it out
together.

*Weak. I shouldn't have to lean on a man for
strength. I should be strong enough to stand on
my own.*

Especially since Roman's solution would un-
doubtedly be to try to convince her to sell the business and let it become someone else's problem.

For the first time, she was actually tempted.
She'd been shouldering the burden alone for so
long. It was no one's fault but her own that both
the shelter and gym were in danger of going

under. Running either of them was a full-time job and Allie was trying to do both by herself. If she'd just been willing to find a business partner she could trust…

At twenty-two, she'd been sure that the only person she could trust was herself. She'd needed some way to work through her grief over her mother passing, and this seemed like the best option. She *was* doing good; it just wasn't working like the well-oiled machine she'd anticipated. *There has to be a better way.* She just didn't know what it was.

Frustrated, she headed out. The evening classes were already covered, so there was nothing holding her there except a strange sort of guilt. There had to be something *more* she could be doing, but hell if she knew what it was. Maybe if she scrambled, she could throw together a fund-raiser or two this month, before it was too late. It would mean relying on her girls to run the gym while she devoted herself to event planning, which had never been her strong suit. Making cold calls to the few donors who'd helped her get the shelter off the ground was the next step, but it had always made her feel awkward and shameful—like she was begging for charity. As it was, her presence at the gym was totally and completely unnecessary at that moment, and all she'd accomplish by staying was working herself further into a spiral of worry.

Allie went upstairs to her apartment. She took her time showering and getting ready, battling nerves that told her this date was a giant waste of time and would only end in heartbreak for her. Roman had his eye on the prize—and the prize wasn't her. It was her gym and the investor interested in it.

Knowing that didn't douse the slow excitement building in her stomach at the thought of seeing him again. It hadn't even been forty-eight hours and she already longed for his touch. *Dangerous*.

She checked the time and decided that being a little early wasn't a bad thing. Nerves were in danger of getting the best of her as she made her way to the restaurant, but she knew Roman well enough at this point to know that he'd find a way to get ahold of her if she no-showed him. What was more, he wouldn't make the same offer twice. This was her chance to get what she wanted—freedom.

Too bad the thought of that didn't fill her with the expected relief. Free meant she wouldn't be seeing Roman again. How could she when he represented such a different set of priorities than she had? Even if she was willing to give it a shot, their respective schedules would mean dates were few and far in between. If things didn't fall apart because of their differences, they'd fall apart because neither one of them could come up with the time to make it work.

Wow. Talk about being fatalistic.

No, I'm being realistic.

She walked into the restaurant Roman had chosen. It wasn't one she was familiar with, and she stopped just inside the door to take it all in. Everything was very modern and minimalist, which was a far cry from the shabby beach chic clutter of West Island. Nothing about the choice screamed Roman to her, but that could very well be because she didn't know him nearly as well as she would have liked to pretend. *You're seesawing all over the place. Get ahold of yourself.*

She told the waitress she was meeting Roman Bassani and was led back to a little booth tucked into the side wall facing the street. The windows weren't big, but they offered plenty of fodder for people watching. Or they would if she could look anywhere but at Roman's perfect face. He rose to meet her, and she couldn't help comparing this man with the one she'd felt so connected to on the island. *Her* Roman was there, beneath the expensive suit and the perfectly styled hair. She could see a hint of him in those hazel eyes, but even the way he held his shoulders was different here. Harsher.

"Hey." She wrapped her arms around herself,

wishing she'd worn something fancier. But that wasn't Allie any more than the relaxed guy in the cargo shorts was Roman. Her wrap dress was nice, but if she didn't miss her guess, he could pay her rent for several months with that suit.

"Hey." He took her hand and pulled her gently closer. The quick kiss he dropped on her lips made her heart ache because it was different, too. Cursory. Distracted. Lacking the heat she'd grown used to that was present in even the smallest of touches between them before.

She disengaged her hand, forced a smile and slid into her seat. "You look nice."

"You're stealing my line." His lips quirked up as he sat across from her. "How was your day?"

Horrible. I can't pay my bills. I'm realizing I care about you a whole lot more than I expected, and the writing is on the wall that both this budding relationship and my ownership of my gym will end awfully. I'm in a funk I don't know that I'll ever get out of. She tried to smile. "It was okay."

Roman's brows slanted down. "What's the truth, Aphrodite? Because that's not it."

She tensed. "Let it go. Please." The last thing Allie wanted to do was rip herself open for him. She didn't do that for *anyone*. She was the strong one. The one who got through things that would break other people and came out the other side swinging with everything she had. It couldn't be clearer that this dinner was the end. Roman wanted things she couldn't give him—and she wasn't talking about her gym and the shelter. He wanted parts of *her*.

No way.

She gritted her teeth and resolved to get to the end of this date so she could secure Roman's promise to leave her business the hell alone. Then she'd walk. Better to end things here and now instead of letting them drag on and enact any one of the horrible scenarios she'd tortured herself with earlier.

The waitress appeared to take their drink order, and Allie was pathetically grateful for the distraction. She ordered a white wine and Roman had whiskey. Then the woman was gone and there was nothing to stand between them. She took a steadying breath. "I'm ready for your pitch."

CHAPTER SIXTEEN

ROMAN STARED AT Allie across the table from him, feeling like he was on a boat headed for a storm, watching the receding shore of paradise and knowing he'd never see it again. Regardless of what she'd told him when she'd agreed to this date, it was clear she'd already made up her mind about both his proposal and him. It made him want to shake her, to force her to see that good things were within reach if she'd just lower the barriers the slightest bit.

If she'd let him in.

He sat back. Might as well get this over with, because he could already see that she wouldn't let him get anywhere near anything personal until they'd both fulfilled their part of the bargain connected to her beloved gym. "I don't have to tell you about the stats of women who feel harassed in their gyms, let alone their daily lives. With Transcend you've created a unique hook that my investor thinks will go over well as a small franchise. Something exclusive to a handful of big cities at first—LA, San Antonio, Seattle, Atlanta, Chicago. Boutique gyms are in right now, but this has the potential to last longer than the fad does, especially if there's some kind of health plan and smoothie bar that goes hand in hand with it."

"That's not what Transcend is about."

"That's exactly what Transcend is about. You are a bastion of safety for women. They flock to that gym because it's one of the few places they can let their guard down a little. *You* are the reason they feel safe, and the little community you've created." He leaned forward and braced his forearms on the table. "Don't women outside this city deserve that feeling, too?"

She met his gaze directly. "There are other women-only gyms out there. Mine is far from unique."

"But yours is the only one connected with a shelter for battered women." This was it. He'd lose her or have her based on this last part. "My investor is interested in continuing and expanding the work you do with the shelter." The hope in her eyes killed him, so he spoke quickly. "With the caveat that you sign over the nonprofit entirely."

"What?"

No use pussyfooting around it. "It's not your passion. The brainchild was all yours, but the delivery has been lackluster at best. You help those women, and *that* is your passion, combined with the gym. But a successful nonprofit requires shmoozing and networking, and that's a full-time job—a job it couldn't be clearer you are not interested in. You haven't done much with it up to this point."

"That's not fair. I—"

He held up a hand. "That wasn't a criticism. You're running two full-time businesses by yourself. It's natural that things have fallen through the cracks as a result. My point—my investor's point—is that if you delegate and hand off a few things, the whole operation could expand and run smoother as a result."

Allie sat back, the golden tone of her skin going pale with worry. "Even if I was interested in signing away everything I've worked for, what guarantee would I have that this investor of yours wouldn't turn around and do exactly the opposite of what they're proposing now?"

"It's something that could be stipulated in the contract." He found himself holding his breath while she seemed to think it over.

But she shook her head. "No. I can't risk it. Those women depend on me to keep them safe, and I don't know a single damn thing about this investor of yours. I've seen how flimsy paperwork can be when it comes to protection—might often makes right, and your investor has all of it."

She was technically right—even with the protections written into the contract, there were limits to what Allie could demand—but Roman knew this investor and he knew that the offer was legit. He wouldn't have fielded it otherwise. "Trust me. I wouldn't have brought this to you, especially after the last week, if I didn't think it would honor what's important to you."

"You keep saying that—to trust you. You haven't done a single thing to earn this level of trust."

And fuck, that stung. He'd shared things with her last week that he didn't talk about with anyone. Even though Allie was still guarded, he'd thought she'd shared shit with him, too. He wasn't a sappy romantic, but that *meant* something.

Or at least, he'd thought it had.

Roman forced the tension from his shoulders. "I have only your best—"

"No."

He waited for some kind of explanation, something he could work with, some sign that she wasn't just shutting him out without explanation. None came. With a slow sinking in his stomach, he sat back. "And if I ask you on another date— if I want this to go somewhere—am I going to get the same answer?"

Allie fiddled with her fork and then set it aside. "I'm sorry, Roman, but I just don't see how this could possibly work out. We're too different."

A nice pat explanation—and it was bullshit. "How are we supposed to give this a shot if you won't talk to me? If you *never* talk to me. You came to dinner tonight with your responses already planned out. It didn't matter what I said, because you were always going to tell me no to investing in the gym, and no to us dating."

She flinched. "I'm saying no to your investor because I don't trust their intentions. And there is no *us*. I had a wonderful time with you on West Island, but that wasn't reality. This?" She motioned between them. "This is reality. You in your expensive suit and me in my secondhand dress. I do whatever I can to help people, and you hurt them *for your job*. We're just too different."

"That's bullshit and you know it." Frustration grabbed him by the throat. She was determined to see the worst in his choice of career, no matter what evidence he provided to the contrary. It didn't matter if he laid out a list of all the happy business owners who had benefited from him doing his job—Allie would pick out the one from the bunch who was pissed and then use it as proof that he was a monster. "You're being a chickenshit. Newsflash, Allie—I'm not your father. I'm as far from that bastard as a man can get, but if you can't see that, then maybe you're right—we don't stand a chance."

Roman wasn't saying anything Allie hadn't said to herself, but somehow hearing those words—that condemnation—come out of his mouth sucked all the air out of the room. "That's not fair."

"Neither is sacrificing a potential future with me because you're scared." He spoke low and fiercely, and part of her wanted to give in and just let him take the wheel. Roman was more than capable of taking care of both of them and guiding the relationship toward…

What am I thinking?

She knew what came from having to depend on a man. Even if Roman would never hurt her—and he wouldn't—he was too overpowering and overwhelming. He would swallow her whole and all that would be left of her identity would be connected to him. Roman's woman.

Not Allie, strong and mostly confident business owner who didn't need to lean on anyone. That person would be gone, and she'd never be able to get her back.

If Allie didn't have her gym, she didn't have anything. She'd be starting over from scratch, selling her soul in the process. It was easy for Roman to tell her to trust him, to talk to him, when *she* was the one making all the sacrifices and he was making none.

"Is that what you really think?"

She hadn't realized she'd spoken all those thoughts aloud, but she'd put it out there and she wasn't about to take it back now. "Isn't that the truth?" Roman had all the chips in this scenario—he had since they'd met. *No, not since we met. That first night, we were on equal footing.* There was no going back now, though. They were who they were, and neither of them could really change that.

He clenched his jaw hard enough that she feared for his teeth. "Talk. To. Me."

"That's exactly what I've been doing this whole time. Just because I'm not saying what you like doesn't mean I'm wrong." She slid out of the booth and stood. "This was a mistake."

"Allie, if you walk out that door, that's it. I'm not going to chase your ass down just so I can keep bashing my head against the same damn wall." He said it with such finality, her throat burned and her eyes prickled.

Because this was it. They'd been hurtling toward this moment since the first time they'd realized each other's identities. Part of her had thought they'd find a way around, but he was too uncompromising, too sure that he knew what was best for her.

And he was right—he was nothing like her father or the abusive men who drove the women to her shelter in flocks. Roman would never hurt someone like that, no matter how angry. She'd stake her life on it.

No, the damage he dealt wasn't physical. It wasn't even intentional. That didn't stop her from feeling like he'd reached into her chest and ripped out her heart. "Goodbye, Roman."

"Allie, wait."

Her feet stopped, even as her brain demanded she keep moving. Almost against her will, she turned and looked at him.

Roman stood and glanced around them. She'd been vaguely aware that they had an audience before then, but the reality of the situation came crashing down on her. She was having a very public breakup with a man who wasn't even her boyfriend. *This is what my life has come to.* "If you have anything left to say, now's the time." She waited, holding her breath, wondering if maybe he'd say something that would override her fears and put them back on something resembling solid ground.

He stepped closer and lowered his voice. The warmth was gone from his eyes, leaving the cold businessman in his place. "If you don't take this investor's offer, you'll be sentencing both your gym and the shelter to death."

Allie flinched. She knew that she was in trouble better than anyone, but that didn't mean she'd put the women who depended on her at risk. Not until she'd exhausted all other options. "I'll find another way."

"Good fucking luck." He shook his head and walked around her. "I do mean that, Allie. It'll take a goddamn miracle to save you at this point, and you just turned down the helping hand I offered. That's on you—not me."

She watched him walk away, a pit opening up inside her with no end. Allie had hit so many snags since she'd set herself on the goal of opening her own business and nonprofit, and every single one of them she'd fought her way through. By all rights she should be furious at Roman, and that should drive her to figure out a solution to this problem.

But all she wanted to do was go home and cry herself to sleep.

She turned to pay for their drinks but caught sight of a fifty that Roman had left on the table. Even pissed as hell, he had ensured that he held up his end of the bargain, at least when it came to this. *Stop thinking about that.* She'd given him the only answer she could. Ultimately, his investor could paint whatever pretty picture they wanted, because when push came to shove, money talked. Once the papers were signed and Allie was no longer in control, the investor could do as they pleased and she'd have no power to stop them.

She'd made the right call. She was sure of it.

She just didn't know why it felt so freaking awful to have pulled the proverbial trigger and put an end to both the investor talk and her time with Roman. She should be relieved. It was over. She'd held up her end of the bargain, and she was free. Not to mention a vacation for the record books, the kind she'd remember fondly for as long as she lived...

Even if all she felt right at that moment was overwhelming sadness.

Allie left the restaurant, thought about grabbing a cab and ultimately decided to walk. She needed to expend some energy, to work her way through the crap circling in her head. Roman's words kept ringing through her mind, telling her that she'd never figure out how to save her gym and the shelter on her own. That she was destined for failure.

Fuck that.

It was easier to focus on business than to deal with the yawning chasm of loss taking up residence in her chest. It didn't matter how much she told herself that she and Roman would never work—she'd secretly hoped that he'd have a solution that would take care of her fears. *Depending on Roman to shoulder all of that was totally fair.* It wasn't that… Allie shook her head and picked up her pace. Maybe it was partly that. She didn't want to depend on him for everything—for anything—but she had still kind of been on the verge of doing exactly that. *Weak.*

She couldn't afford to be weak. Not in business, and not in her yearning for Roman.

Allie still had to fight not to call him as she strode down the block toward her apartment. She wanted to talk to him, to yell, or cry, or…something. Connect. She'd been adrift for so long, and she hadn't realized it until his grounding presence had slammed into her life. The fact they'd spent only a week together should have been a bucket of cold water on her, but it didn't seem to make any difference. They had a connection, and it scared her. It didn't seem to scare him as much, but what did he have to lose? The scales of their risk were not equal.

Roman would move on with his life after this. She had no illusions that he'd be happy to leave her behind, but he was a driven individual who wouldn't let a little heartache stop him from reaching his goals. He'd find a better-fitting investment for this client. And the next, and the next.

Eventually he'd start dating. Even as chaotic as his schedule had to be, he was too much of the full package *not* to find a woman willing to put up with it. They'd date the appropriate amount of time and then he'd propose on an island a whole lot like West Island. Hell, maybe he'd actually propose *there*.

The thought made her sick to her stomach.

Just get home. You can break down when you get home.

She flagged down a cab and rattled off her address. Through the entire drive, Allie focused on breathing, putting every bit of concentration she had on that single task. It got her as far as her front door and then she slumped to the floor. "Oh, God, what am I going to do?"

CHAPTER SEVENTEEN

"YOU'RE IN A pissy-ass mood."

Roman stared at his drink. It was his second, and he forced himself to sip it instead of shooting it like he wanted to. No matter how good of a friend the man next to him was, he still couldn't afford to lose control. *Mostly because I'll end up drunk texting Allie and making a damn fool of myself.* "I'm fine."

Aaron Livingston snorted. "You're about as far from fine as a man gets. I've never seen you this out of sorts about a deal falling through."

The deal and Allie were all twisted up in his head, and he couldn't untangle them. That investor would have *helped* her. He couldn't divulge details until the contracts were set, but his client, Clare Belford, was the perfect fit for that company. She had one of the biggest nonprofits for abused women in the country, and she'd loved the idea of Allie's gym being linked up with several of them.

Because of a nondisclosure agreement he had with Clare, he hadn't been able to tell Allie that, but if she'd just trusted him, she would have found out shortly.

Except she hadn't trusted him.

He was good enough to fuck, but anything beyond that was strictly off-limits. The thought had him downing the rest of his drink despite his best intentions. He motioned to the bartender to refill the glass, doing his best to ignore the curious look he could feel Aaron giving him. "I don't want to talk about it."

"Holy fuck." Aaron leaned against the bar, blue eyes narrowed. "It's not business at all— it's woman trouble."

"What part of 'I don't want to talk about it' don't you get?"

"You do want to talk about it. You wouldn't be here otherwise." Aaron waited for the bartender to slide the newly filled glass over before continuing. "You weren't seeing anyone before you left for the island, and that place has a limited population of guests, so there was only one woman there who'd be twisting you up like this." He whistled softly. "You and Allie Landers? I thought you didn't mix business with pleasure."

"I don't—didn't." He eyed his glass but didn't pick it up.

"You might as well get it off your chest. I can't say I've ever had that look on my face, but I have three sisters, so I know a thing or two about women."

Roman almost commented on the fact that if he had to recall his sisters for advice instead of his own dating history, he wasn't much help. But the truth was that Roman had a varied dating history and he'd never been this fucked up over a woman. Even his worst breakups and the respective aftermaths had been filled with a sense of peace because it was the right call.

There was no peace in this.

He nudged his glass farther away. "I had all the answers. The solution to everything she needed. All I got for my trouble was a kick in the ass as she showed me the door." When Aaron made a noncommittal noise, he kept going. "I never planned on her. Fuck, man, she's strong and gorgeous and smart as hell. I'm talking full package. I thought we were on the same wavelength, but she didn't even try to see that I might actually be right. She's so determined to do things her way, she won't even give us a shot."

"You want the bro-supportive view or real talk?"

He finally looked at Aaron. Roman could have

called Gideon to come drink with him, but his other friend was so deep in his romantic bliss with Lucy Baudin that he wouldn't be able to commiserate. Aaron, at least, was single. All Roman had really wanted was someone to drink with who wouldn't press too hard, but he'd underestimated Aaron. It was tempting to say he wanted the supportive viewpoint, but Roman had never shied away from the shitty side of things, so he went with the hard truth option. "The latter."

"You fucked up."

He blinked. "How do you figure?"

"Look at this from her perspective—you crashed her vacation and, yeah, maybe your intense chemistry made everything else take a back seat for the week, but nothing really changed. You were still the conquering enemy force once you two got back to New York. You have the standard contract with the prospective investor?"

"Yeah. Always."

Aaron nodded. "So even if it's the best fit, you aren't telling her shit about this person and you're expecting her to just take your word for it. From all accounts, Allie Landers is a woman who's been holding the world on her shoulders and dealing with every issue that's arisen on her own. You can't seriously have expected her to just flip on a dime and put everything she's worked years for on the line on your word alone."

"I expected her to trust me," Roman snapped. The fact she hadn't still stung like a bitch.

"Why?"

He growled. "Because I would never hurt her or what she cares about."

"Maybe you know that. Maybe she even knows that on some level." Aaron shrugged. "If your delivery was anything similar to the one you've given tonight, you can't blame her for telling you to fuck off. Maybe the sex changed things for you both, but if you didn't tell her that, how's she supposed to know? She's not a damn mind reader."

He wanted to rail at his friend—at Allie—that she should have trusted him anyway, but... What had he really done to earn that trust? A multitude of orgasms was great, but it didn't translate—a fact he damn well knew. He'd opened up about his past a bit, but he hadn't exactly made himself overly vulnerable to her. He'd held back. They might have established a connection, but it certainly didn't earn him the amount of trust he could expect her to stake her business on. He drank some of his whiskey, forcing himself to go slow. "I care about her."

"And it's making you stupid. Don't worry— you're not the only one who's done it. She made mistakes in this, too, but we're not talking about her. We're talking about you." Aaron took a pull of his beer. "The question remains—what the hell are you going to do about it?"

Allie cared about him. Roman would bet everything he owned on that fact. His pride might be demanding he let the whole thing go and move on with his life...but he couldn't wrap his mind around moving on from this. Allie was special. More than what he felt for her, he wanted her to succeed in the vision she'd put into play. He wanted to be by her side when she saw it realized. If he walked now, he wouldn't do any of that.

What was his pride when compared with his happiness—and hers?

He checked his watch and stood. "I'm going to go get my girl."

"There you go." Aaron toasted him with his beer. "Though I'd recommend waiting for morning, since it's after ten."

Roman was already turning for the door. "I have a few calls to make. I'll catch up with you later." He had several things to line up before he could talk to Allie. If he wanted a chance to succeed in winning her back, he had to be able to present new information—to change the narrative.

A pounding on the door brought Allie out of her light doze. She shot to her feet before she realized that she wasn't in her bed, and nearly tripped over the coffee table. She scrubbed a hand over her face and headed for the door as whoever was on the other side kept knocking. For one crazy moment she was sure it was Roman, coming to find her after last night to say… She didn't know what. Something.

But when she opened the door, it was Becka on the other side. Her friend took one look at her and shook her head. "Oh, God. It's worse than I thought."

"What?"

Becka nudged her back into the apartment and shut the door. "You. You are worse than I thought. Look at you—you're wearing holey sweats, you have powdered sugar on your shirt and there are ink stains all over your hands. Something is going on with you, and I want to know what it is. Did Roman do something? Do I need to kick his ass to Brooklyn and back?"

"What? No." *Yes. Sort of.* She smoothed her hair back, belatedly realizing that she hadn't showered today and her messy bun was more mess than bun. "Roman and I had a vacation fling and it's over now."

Becka narrowed her eyes. "Bullshit."

"Excuse me?"

"You heard me. You were well on your way to head over heels for that guy, and from the way he looked at you, he was right there with you. So what gives? Because you were fine when we flew back to the city, and now you're on the verge of a breakdown."

She opened her mouth to make some excuse and change the subject just like she always did when Becka put her on the spot, but despair got the better of her. "I'm in trouble, Becka. Big trouble."

Instantly, her friend's half-joking demeanor disappeared. "Tell me so we can fix it."

"I don't know if there's any fixing this." She walked back to the couch and sat down, waiting for Becka to join her before she started in. Allie detailed how far behind they were on bills, how she'd been borrowing from her own income to supplement both the gym and the shelter, how she was almost drained dry.

How she'd told Roman no even though he'd offered her a potential way out.

"Well, yeah." Becka nodded. "He didn't give you much in the way of assurances, and I get why you said no." Before Allie could relax, she continued. "What I don't get is why this is the first time I'm hearing about all this."

"I thought I could handle it." Even when she'd realized she couldn't, putting that burden on someone else went against everything Allie was. She was the problem solver, and she knew she could depend on herself. *Other people* depended on her—she didn't depend on other people. She didn't know how to reach out when she was in trouble.

Becka gave her a look. "You know, it's not the worst thing in the world to ask for help. You're allowed to not be perfect."

"I know I'm not perfect."

She snorted. "But you don't know how to lean on other people. As your best friend, I'm all about blindly hating anyone you hate, but I have a question and I want you to answer it honestly."

Even knowing where this was going, she couldn't help nodding. "Okay."

"Did you even stop to consider for a second that maybe Roman was on the up-and-up? That maybe he cared about you and was telling the truth about his investor and he only wanted to help?" She held up a hand. "I mean, the man is not a saint. He went after this account because he knew it would make his investor happy, and he didn't really care about what you wanted before he met you—but that doesn't mean that the investor is an evil mastermind who wants to destroy everything you've worked toward. Did you ask Roman if you were going to be able to stay on in any capacity?"

"No." Heat climbed her chest and throat to settle in her face. Embarrassment. "He wanted me to compromise on everything and just have faith that he wasn't screwing me. I just…reacted."

Becka nodded. "I mean, I'm not saying you were 100 percent in the wrong. He played that poorly from beginning to end. But I also think that maybe, just maybe, you reacted instead of thinking it through. I know you want to be able to do this all yourself, but there's no shame in letting someone else share your vision—and help you realize it."

She took a slow breath. "All those women are depending on me to help them."

"Whoa. Slow down there, Wonder Woman. Those women are grateful for a safe space, yes, but they're not helpless. They're not children who need you to see to their every need. You can't put all that on your shoulders." She leaned forward. "Let's be honest here for a second, okay?"

Allie managed a half smile. "We weren't being honest before now?"

"You know what I mean. I love the shit out of you, but you can be bullheaded to a clinical degree. Roman scared you. He made you feel things and he offered you something you want desperately but are afraid to take because it might blow up in your face. I get that. I do. But I also think you latched on to any reason why it wouldn't work and just ran with it, ignoring any indication that you might be—just maybe—dead wrong."

She didn't want to admit that. Roman was as bullheaded as she was—if not more so. She couldn't afford to show weakness because he'd steamroll her.

Except by not showing weakness, she'd put them in a position where it was all or nothing. There was no compromise because *she* hadn't tried to compromise. She'd just turned him down and cut things off because it was easier than putting herself out there and trying. Becka's words wouldn't smart so much if they didn't have more than a grain of truth in them. "Damn it, you're right."

"I often am." Becka slouched back onto the couch and pulled her legs up to her chest. "So, to simplify—you like Roman a whole hell of a lot, and you're in trouble with the gym—the kind of trouble an investor would solve, but only the right investor."

"That about sums it up." She twisted a lock of hair around her finger. "I guess if I had the right investor, it wouldn't be hard to sign over control—at least partial control. Someone who has the same vision I do, and who wants the same things."

"That makes sense." Becka grinned. "Good thing we know someone with a whole list of people wanting to invest in start-up companies that have promise. I imagine if you went to Roman with a counteroffer, he'd fall all over himself to give you whatever you want."

Since Allie couldn't imagine a scenario where Roman fell all over himself, she just nodded. She could go to a different person to make this connection, but that seemed the height of stupidity—and cowardice. Facing Roman and admitting that she was wrong shouldn't be the end of the world. It wouldn't be comfortable, but what if he really had been serious about giving them a real shot? She'd spend the rest of her life wondering if she'd missed the love of her life because she was too stubborn to ask for help. "I should call him, huh?"

"If you think so."

She considered it for a full thirty seconds. "I'm going to shower and *then* I'm going to go find him."

"That's my girl!"

CHAPTER EIGHTEEN

ALLIE'S INTENTIONS WERE all well and good, but she couldn't find Roman. He wasn't in his office, and no one seemed to know what his schedule was—and he hadn't answered any of her calls. By the time the afternoon rolled around, she was on the verge of despair. *Maybe I misread the entire situation and he really wasn't interested beyond the gym and now he wants nothing to do with me.*

Not sure what else to do, she sent him a quick text. I'm sorry. I'd like to talk. Can we meet somewhere?

Her phone buzzed before she had a chance to set it down. Where are you?

He wouldn't respond to any of her calls, but he responded to a text—because of course. Down was up and up was down, just like it had been since she'd met Roman. The gym.

Stay there. On my way.

Her heart leaped into her throat and she had to swallow several times before she was able to force her thumbs to type out a reply. Okay.

She tried to busy herself with paperwork, but she kept watching the clock and wondering what was going on. Allie wanted to talk, for sure, but Roman's abrupt texts made her wonder all over again if this was a mistake.

No. Stop it. You care about him, and you're going to fight for him, damn it.

She clung to that thought for the next twenty-five minutes. When someone knocked on her office door, she nearly bolted out of her chair. "Come in!"

Roman walked through, and the sight of him was like coming home. He wore a pair of dark slacks and a button-down shirt that did wonders for his shoulders, and the look he gave her when he breached the door was one of a returning hero. As if he had craved the sight of her as much as she'd wanted him.

She opened her mouth to say all the things she'd had running through her head for the last day, but stopped when she registered that he wasn't alone. A petite silver-haired woman stepped into the room. Her face was ageless enough that Allie couldn't tell if her silver hair was trendy or all natural, but she could only be termed a handsome woman. Her bone structure was a little too strong to be merely pretty, and she carried herself with a confidence that filled the room.

Roman shut the door and turned to Allie. "I'd like to introduce you to Clare Belford—the investor who hired me."

She froze. "I know that name… You're the woman who runs Safe Places."

"I am." Clare's voice was low and melodious. "I'm really impressed with the operation you're running."

"I— Thank you. I love your work. You make such a difference in so many women's lives."

Clare moved closer to her desk. "Roman here told me about your concerns—which are perfectly valid—and I wanted to meet you to reassure you that I have every intention of staying true to your vision. I would like to incorporate your shelter into Safe Places and expand Transcend to pair new gyms with the current shelters in the cities Roman suggested. And I would also like to hire you to stay on as general manager of both the local shelter and the original gym. I know it's not the same thing as owner, but I'm prepared to allow you full autonomy provided you operate within the parameters you've already established."

Allie couldn't breathe. She couldn't think. It was everything she could do not to cry. In all her imaginings of how things would go down with her shelter and gym, *this* wasn't even on the list of possibilities. She cleared her throat. "That sounds wonderful."

"Don't give me an answer now. Think it over and let me know by the end of the week." Clare reached out and shook Allie's hand. Her grip was just as confident as her personality. "I'm glad we were able to meet."

"Me, too."

Roman waited for the door to close behind Clare to speak. "I'm sorry."

She still couldn't quite process the turn of events. "I thought you couldn't talk about who your investor was."

"I signed a nondisclosure agreement. It's standard because the job can get a little sticky when it comes to negotiations and some investors would rather not be identified beforehand for their own reasons."

The dots connected with a snap she could almost hear. "You asked her to talk to me."

He hesitated. "While it would have been great if you'd trusted me on this, I understand why you didn't now. You have more than just your life at stake, and going into the situation with only my word isn't sufficient. I knew if you met with Clare, you would understand that this will only mean good things for both the shelter and the gym—and more women than you can reach on your own."

Allie took a breath, and then another. "Roman, I don't know what to say."

"Then just… I have to apologize—actually apologize. I was pissed that you wouldn't trust me, but I was asking you to do all the bending and I wasn't putting anything on the line to keep us on equal footing. So here it is—I love you, Aphrodite. I know it's too soon and you have reservations, but I'm willing to do whatever it takes to be with you. If that means you need time, then I'll give you as much time as you need." The tense look on his face conveyed how much he liked that idea, but he charged on. "We can go as fast or as slow as you want, but *I* want *you*. So unless you don't want me back, this is happening."

God, she was more than a little in love with him, too.

Allie stood and rounded the desk to stand in front of him. "If we're going to restart this on the right foot, I have to apologize, too. I went with my knee-jerk reaction to take care of things myself and didn't stop to think that maybe it's okay to lean on someone or to ask for help." She shifted closer to him, not quite willing to touch him yet, but wanting to. "I was actually calling you today to ask if you'd help set me up with an investor."

She smiled. "I guess we were on the same page, after all."

Roman took her hands, his expression serious. "If you aren't comfortable with what Clare is offering, we can find someone else. I'm not going to push you on this. I promise."

"I'm going to take her offer." She'd known it the second Clare had made it. As much as it had initially been her dream to own her own business, being the GM wasn't much of a step down. If she was able to keep control and be assured that all the women who came through her shelter were cared for... It was worth it. It was more than worth it. "Thank you. I'm sorry I didn't trust you."

"You have nothing to apologize for."

She slipped into his arms. "I do have one other thing to say."

"Just one?" A smile flirted with the edges of his lips.

"I love you, too." She kissed him, showing him she meant the words, putting everything she felt into the contact. "This might be too soon, and it might be a little crazy, but I wouldn't have it any other way."

* * * * *

COMING SOON!

We really hope you enjoyed reading this book. If you're looking for more romance, be sure to head to the shops when new books are available on

Thursday
26th July

To see which titles are coming soon, please visit
millsandboon.co.uk

LET'S TALK
Romance

For exclusive extracts, competitions
and special offers, find us online:

f facebook.com/millsandboon

⊙ @millsandboonuk

🐦 @millsandboon

Or get in touch on 0844 844 1351*

For all the latest titles coming soon, visit
millsandboon.co.uk/nextmonth